Someone Like Me

Brittni Huyck

To the dreamers of the world and the believers in soulmates... this one's for you.

Prologue

Have you ever been in love?

Like the overwhelming, all consuming, mind numbing good love?

When you find the one that you know you want to spend the rest of your days with. It's the only person you can't imagine not falling asleep and waking up next to.

The one individual that you know was made for you… your soulmate, your other half, your rock, the love of your life.

Not many people get to really feel the intensity of finding the exact person that was created for them. Then getting to spend eternity making memories and just truly living.

I feel bad for these people.

I feel bad that they will never know what it feels like to look into someone's eyes and see forever staring back.

Fortunately for them, they will also never have to feel the pain of finally finding their person, only to watch them walk away. Taking their heart and every ounce of their colorful outlook on life with them.

As I sit here, a broken shell of the person that I once knew, I can't help but think… maybe they're the lucky ones.

Chapter 1

Halee

Four months earlier... May

    I'm currently sitting across the living room from my best friend, who continues to gush over her seemingly perfect fiancé. All while we're supposed to be talking about their future wedding plans. This isn't bitterness in my voice. I'm truly happy for her, she deserves all the happiness in the world after everything she's been through.

    Quinn was once in love and engaged to another man, her high school sweetheart, but everything changed the day he ran into a structure fire. He never came back out. I shouldn't be jealous of her, I know this. No one should ever have to endure the amount of pain and heartache she has.

    My envy doesn't come from her pain.

It stems from the fact that she has not only had one great love, but two.

A year ago, I never thought anyone or anything would bring her out of the destructive state she was in after Brett died, but then came Walker. His six-foot-two body covered in muscles and tattoos came strolling into town. Just like that, everything in her world was right again.

I know people say that things happen for a reason, and it seems super shitty to think Brett died so she could meet Walker. But I think that's exactly what happened. She has a lightness about her now that I'd never seen with Brett, almost like things come easier for the two of them and the world is spinning exactly as it should be. Two soul mates found their way to each other, and here I am, on like relationship number one hundred and I can't seem to find a decent guy to save my life.

Over the years it feels like I have tried just about everything to meet a good guy. Even those crazy dating apps where you swipe left or right depending on what you are looking for. That was a joke, the only thing those guys were looking for was a quick lay and then they moved onto the next willing participant.

I don't feel like I have unrealistic expectations, a nice guy, family and goal oriented, active, someone who can make me laugh, doesn't take life too seriously and most importantly, can have a good time. But date after date that I go on just continues to be a let down.

The guy I was out with last week asked me to come back to his place so we could hang out and get to know each other better, but informed me as we were walking out of the restaurant that we had to keep it down because his mom is a light sleeper.

Thanks, but no thanks.

This all led me here, giving up on the idea of any near future relationships and accepting my role as the permanent third wheel to these two love birds.

"You two are annoyingly cute. I think I'm going to take off before I become even more depressed about my current lack of a love life."

Quinn peels her attention away from Walkers face and gives me a look of sympathy, "Sorry, Hales. I've been meaning to ask, how did your date last week go? You said that he seemed promising."

I let out a laugh remembering the look on that guys face when I told him I was suddenly experiencing explosive diarrhea and had to head home. "He was promising on paper and the date was great. In fact, he was basically ready for me to move in with him… and his mother. I faked a case of diarrhea and got out of there before he could ask about another date. Honestly I've been ignoring his calls since."

Walker laughs and looks up from whatever wedding pamphlet Quinn had him looking at, "You mean to tell me that you told this man you had a case of the shits, and he called you for a follow up?"

His hysterical belly laughing continues as Quinn chimes back in, "Yea Hales, maybe he is a decent guy."

"He absolutely IS a decent guy, but he also lives with his mother. And not because she's ill or because he needed a place to stay until he could get back on his feet. He straight up told me, 'It's like having a roommate that cooks for you and does your laundry'. No thank you, that's asking for trouble. I want an independent man who can take care of himself, not someone who will instantly be expecting me to take the place of his mother. Or worse, move in with the two of them so she can do my laundry and cook for me." Although looking back at the idea, I guess I can see the perks.

I wave my hand at them, "Anyways, I've decided to take a step back from the dating scene and focus on me for awhile. Maybe I've just been trying too hard and putting too much energy into finding someone. But enough about me, let's get back to this wedding planning. What's next on the list?"

Quinn's face lights up and she looks over to Walker and then back to me, slightly jumping up and down in her seat. "I've actually been meaning to talk to you about that, Walker has a friend that's a country singer. He's playing about two hours from here this weekend at a bar, I want to go check him out and see if he has the right feel for what we are looking for, but Walker can't go. He's covering a shift for one of the guys at the department. Soooo... I was thinking maybe we can make it a girls' night? You, me and Charlie?"

"Why can't you guys be normal and have a DJ like everyone else in the world?"

They both look at me as if I've grown two heads. After I realize that I would not be getting a reply I say, "Sure, count me in, but you better mention it to Charlie so that she can find a babysitter for Tuck."

"Already taken care of, JR offered to hang out with him for the night." Walker says. "He has a serious hard on for that girl, I'm pretty sure he would hang himself by his dick in the middle of winter if she'd asked."

Quinn rolls her eyes and elbows him in the ribs, "Ugh, why can't you just say that he likes her? That is such a gross visual. Plus I've told him over and over, she isn't ready to jump into another relationship right now."

When we hired Charlie we didn't know much about her, just that she was new to town, and looking for a fresh start. It wasn't until weeks later that we found out she has a three year old son named Tucker. She'd left southern Indiana because she was running from her piece-of-shit ex who used to hit her. She endured a lot being with him but one day he took it to the next level, laying his hands on Tuck. Charlie called the police and while he was at the station being questioned, she packed up everything she could fit in her car and left.

"I think she could, he just has to give her time. I can't imagine trying to trust someone and let them in after what that asshole put her through." I pause, "Back to our girls' night, tell me about this band. Walker, you know them?"

"Yea." He says as he stands up, heading to the kitchen. "You two want a drink?"

After we nod, he goes on, "Not really a band, just a single guy, his name is Luke. We met a few times in Chicago while I was living there. Super cool dude and seriously talented. He's from the south originally, at least I think, he has quite the southern drawl going on. I already know he's perfect but you know how miss has to control everything gets." He turns his thumb in Quinn's direction and she returns his gaze by sticking her tongue out.

Leaning down he hands us our drinks and kisses Quinn on the forehead. She lets out a dramatic scoff, "I do not need to control everything but the band is a big deal, and it's a great excuse to go out with my girls."

"Hell yeah, we're going to get a little crazy." I fist pump the air.

Chapter 2

Halee

This week seemed to drag on, client after client that couldn't make up their mind on what they wanted. I think my favorite quote from the week was, "I don't care what you do, but I want to look completely different. I need a change, but don't cut anything off and nothing too extreme with the color."

I wanted to say, 'so you want the same color as usual and a trim', but it doesn't work that way. You put your best foot forward and hope they love what you've done in the end.

I knew I wanted to be a stylist since I was a little girl and most days I enjoy it, especially since I get to work alongside my best friend everyday. But lately it all feels different and I don't know why. Maybe it's because I'm not in a good place in my personal life and that seems to roll over into my work. Whatever it is, I need to get my shit together, I've had more than one client ask me if everything is ok. Apparently my over bubbly personality is nonexistent right now, and it takes more effort than normal to carry on basic conversations with people.

All of that is ending today, I'm going to focus on me. Maybe the reason that I can't find someone else to truly make me happy is because I don't feel happy with myself. I think it's time to take a hiatus from guys, a "guyatus". I'm going to become the best possible version of myself so when I find that perfect man, I'm ready for him.

That all starts with girls' night. And I'm beyond excited to get this evening started when my last client walks out the door.

"You bitches ready for tonight?" I yell towards the break room, where Quinn and Charlie have been hanging out since their last clients left. "I just have to change, throw some makeup on and I'll be ready to get out of here."

Quinn walks around the corner from the back room, she's already dressed for our night out in a black flowy summer dress that hits just above her knee, a denim jacket and her go to white Converse. I swear if she wasn't my best friend I would hate her, she is gorgeous, from her piercing emerald eyes, to her natural strawberry blonde hair. "Good, hurry up. It's about a two hour drive and we're already pushing it for time."

I walk out of the bathroom ten minutes later, after deciding to go with my cut off shorts, a bright yellow off the shoulder sweater and my Birkenstocks. The best part of this new adventure of finding myself, is that I don't feel that constant need to be on my "A" game all of the time. Charlie is in the lobby of the salon now with Quinn when I walk in. She's wearing a pair of black skinny jeans, a grey v neck shirt- showing her assets off perfectly, a leather jacket and a pair of strappy black heels.

"Is that really what you are wearing?" Quinn says to me with her eyebrow raised up like she can't believe what she's seeing. "And I thought I was dressing down with my outfit."

"Didn't you say that it's just a bar? Am I underdressed? We can stop at my house on the way so I can change if you think I need to."

Charlie speaks up, "I think you look great Halee. I'm definitely wishing that I would've brought a different pair of shoes for the evening- my feet are going to be screaming at me after a night out in these things."

"Let's get on the road before we miss Luke's show; we're already going to be cutting it close." Quinn says. She swats me on the butt as we walk out the door. "By the way, I like this less dolled up version of my best friend. It just surprised me, it's been years since you have gone out and not spent hours getting ready."

I give her an exaggerated toddler like smile, "Well, let's just say I'm trying to get back to the old Halee. You know the one that could care less what everyone else thinks. I'm going to do me for awhile, take a break from the dating scene and then maybe in a few months I'll be ready to get back out there."

"Shotgun!" Charlie yells, startling me. "And I think that's a fantastic idea Halee, being single isn't that bad. In fact, it's kinda great. You can go to the bar, flirt with guys, get free drinks and the ball is completely in your hands. If you want to take it further great, if not, you simply thank them for the drink and move on to the next. No commitment, it's my new motto."

We pull onto the highway heading north and since we are all stuck in this jeep what better time to question Charlie about JR. "Yea but the difference between you and I, is you have a great guy who's crazy about you and Tuck, who would move oceans to be with you. Yet, you choose to keep him on the sidelines. Are you just not into him? If that's the case you really should let JR in on that little detail."

"Walker said when they were at Stubs the other night, JR had a couple of girls trying to initiate something with him. From the sound of it, he didn't even give them the time of day." Quinn continues, "He said that it was crazy, never has he seen JR act that way. Typically he's all about the attention and the random hookups, but since you came to town all that has stopped."

Charlie puts her face into her hands and lets out a long breath, "It's not that I don't like him, I do. And obviously I find him attractive, I mean you'd have to be blind not to. Especially since every time he comes around he finds a reason to take his darn shirt off. I swear, he came over last week to look at my kitchen sink; I went to go put Tucker in bed and came back out to the kitchen only to find a shirtless JR laying on the floor. He claimed that he got it wet so that's why he had to take it off, but it didn't look wet when he put it back on before he left."

Quinn and I are cracking up laughing. Typical JR, he's always been in shape and has always been more than willing to show that off to whoever would look. We've all been friends since elementary school, and both of us girls look at him more like a brother than anything else. But I can understand where other girls would be attracted to him; he definitely isn't hard on the eyes.

Charlie is still rambling about JR, "...you see, I do like him. A lot actually. I'm just not ready to jump into another relationship, with him or anyone else. The wounds from my ex husband are too fresh, for god sakes our divorce isn't even final yet."

Quinn steps into the role of big sister that she plays so well, "Ok, but if at any point you decide that you don't want anything from him, you have to be honest. I've never seen him so smitten with someone before. Just don't break his heart."

Charlie nods, silently agreeing to everything we've just said.

The rest of our car ride is considerably lighter. We spend most of the drive singing, terribly might I add, along to songs from our high school years. A wide range from Salt-n-Pepa, Ne-Yo, throwing in a few '90s country songs, and of course we know every single word of them by heart. Charlie may not have grown up in the same town as us but I guarantee that if she did, we would have all been best friends.

Chapter 3

Halee

"Bar" seemed to be a bit of an understatement.

Stubs is a bar. This place is a club, and it is jam-packed. There's a line outside stretching down the sidewalk and around the corner of the building. Just as I'm about to complain there is no way in hell that I'm waiting out here to see anyone, let alone a nobody, Quinn starts walking to the front of the line towards the bouncer.

"Ahhh… Quinn, what are you doing? I'm pretty sure the back of the line is back around that corner. And unless Walker's friend Luke is followed by the last name Bryan or Combs, I'm not standing out here all night. We'll just have to figure out another place and time to go see him."

She glances back at me from over her shoulder, gives me one of her 'I've got this covered' winks, walks straight up to the oversized bouncer and whispers something in his ear. Before I can question what the hell she's doing, the large man lifts the rope and waves the three of us inside.

The mass of bodies inside overwhelms me.

We're definitely not in Iron City and this is nothing like Stubs. We make our way towards the main bar, holding onto each others hands so none of us can get lost in the crowd. Once we arrive, I quickly gain the attention of the bartender, shout our order and then turn back towards the girls. "Q, what'd you say to that bouncer out there? You didn't offer him sexual favors in the ladies room at the end of the night, did ya?"

Our tequila shots and beer arrive, we all lift our glasses and cheers to a much needed girls night. I refocus my eyes on Quinn waiting for an answer. "Nah, girl. I told him you'd meet him in the mens room after the show." Just as I was taking a drink of my beer she causes me to choke a little, but not letting it phase her, she winks and continues, "Just kidding Hales, Luke knew we were coming. He put us on the list so we didn't have to wait outside. His manager told him that this was going to be a big turnout and when the guys talked,

Walker said he didn't feel comfortable with us standing outside alone."

That Walker, he really is her knight in shining armor.

Looking around the club, I notice there are three smaller bar areas scattered throughout and a main stage directly in front of us. Turning back to the bartender I ask, "Hey, how much longer until Luke comes on?"

He doesn't stop what he is doing, never making eye contact with me but responds, "You missed his first set, but the intermission is almost over. He'll be back out for one more any time now." Before I can thank him, he takes off back to the other side of the bar to deliver the beer he just poured.

"Did you guys hear that? Looks like we missed his first set but he should be back out soon to do one more." They both nod at me and we decide to make our way towards the stage. The closer we get, the louder the music is and the male to female ratio is decreasing, along with the amount of clothes these women are wearing. "Anyone else feeling overdressed here?" I holler over the noise.

"I might've forgotten to mention that Luke is kinda attractive." Quinn shrugs. "I mean you guys have seen what my man has going on, so I don't think he's anything to write home about, but he's definitely not ugly."

Just then the lights in the bar dim and you can see that someone is back on the stage, but it's so dark all you can make out is a silhouette. Slowly, the stage lights focus in on the most beautiful man I have ever seen in my life, and judging by the screams around me, the other women agree. Charlie and I look at each other quickly and scream "Dibs!" like we are fighting over who gets the biggest bowl of ice cream after dinner.

I turn my attention back to the man on stage only to find his eyes locked with mine. He's sitting on a stool, guitar in his hand, backwards ball cap, wearing a simple black henley that stretches perfectly across his broad chest, dark denim jeans with a hole in one knee and worn looking boots.

This man's a god! A god that's looking at me like he wants to do dirty things to my body. Judging by the wetness that has taken up residency between my legs, my body is craving for him to do it all to me.

He breaks the intense eye contact first and begins his set. Time seems to stand still as I stand there and watch him sing about trucks, mud, getting drunk and other southern man shit. Charlie yanks on my arm, pulling me out of the trance I was in. "Are you just going to stand there and drool over him, or are ya going to dance with us. It's been three songs."

Three songs? Had I been staring at him for that long, he must really think I'm a creep. "I was not drooling, but Walker was right, he is talented. And so, so sexy."

Quinn laughs and continues to sway her hips along to the music, "I'm pretty sure he didn't say he was '*so, so sexy*' but yeah, I think he's pretty good. I have to talk to him after the show, so you'd better wipe your chin and pull yourself together."

I was not drooling, don't get me wrong, he screams sex on a stick and my body is reacting to him in ways that I have never felt before. But I'm on a guyatus. I told myself I was going to take a few months to focus on me. I definitely don't need to throw all of that away for a musician who probably has hundreds of girls throwing themselves at him every night... even if he is a sexy southern rockstar who, with just one look, can soak my panties.

Making it a point not to turn back around, I dance the rest of the set with the girls. Wondering the whole time if his eyes are still on me or if he has moved on to one of the other girls moving her hips along to his music.

Chapter 4

Luke

"Great show, Luke."

My sister Annie's voice pulls me out of the daze I was in. I honestly don't even remember the second half of the set because I was so enamored by the tiny blonde firecracker that shook her body perfectly to the beat of my songs.

I'm not naive to the fact that I am a good looking, southern man, who happens to be crazy talented in the music department. So when equally as good looking women stand in the front row of my shows and gawk at me, I shoot them my typical Luke Taylor panty-dropping-wink and move on to the next set of eyes, or better yet, tits.

But that's where it stops. I have a one night policy when it comes to "groupies". Well, I guess women in general. I don't do two nights, I don't do hearts and flowers, I don't do love. And I'm one hundred percent transparent about all of this.

I let someone in once and let's just say I won't make that mistake again. Fool me once, shame on you, fool me twice… well you know how the saying goes.

"Thanks Annie. You were right, there was one hell of a crowd out there tonight." My mind flashes back to images of *her* grinding her hips, arms above her tight body, sweat dripping down her back. The way that she pulled her hair on top of her head in one of those messy buns that I'm embarrassed to even know about. Most of the women here tonight were in skin tight dresses, hooker heels, and faces caked with makeup, but the first thing I noticed about her was her daisy duke shorts, oversized yellow sweater that dipped low on one of her shoulders and those terribly ugly Jesus sandals that women think are stylish.

And her eyes, I only saw them for a second when the lights hit the crowd, but they're now embedded into my soul. They were as blue as the ocean. Everything about her instantly made me feel like home.

I wipe my face with my towel, "Annie, I have to meet with my buddy Walkers fiancé tonight about playing at their wedding reception. But while I do that, any way you can go look for a tiny blonde chick in shorts and a bright yellow sweater?"

My sisters eyebrow raises so high it about hits her hairline.

Annie's not just my manager and sister, but she's also just about the only woman I trust if I'm being honest. She's a mere sixteen months older than me, but good luck telling her that.

Our mom split after realizing she didn't want two kids under the age of two, leaving our pops to work two jobs and raise us. He did the best he could, given the circumstances but most of the time Annie was left to take care of me and things around the house.

The look on her face is the typical concerned big sister look she gives me before she is about to spew out some unsolicited advice. "What the hell do I look like Luke, your pimp? If you want some groupie slut to bang tonight, you can walk your happy ass out there and pick her up yourself." She lets out an aggravated huff, "I swear, you'll never learn will you? Always thinking with the wrong head. All these girls just want you for one reason… to say they've been with 'the Luke Taylor'".

Throwing my hands in the air like I'm surrendering, "Okay, okay sis… no need to throw a hissy fit. Forget I said anything." I let out a little of my southern drawl that she can't seem to stay mad at and smile. I guess I'll need to go out and find her myself, hopefully she's still here after I finish up with Walker's lady.

Just then, there's a knock on my dressing room door. Annie gets up to answer it; who knows what could be on the other side of that door. This venue has security but you can only imagine the things women will do to get backstage. I once walked into my private quarters at a bar only to find a groupie butt-ass naked, spread eagle sitting on the couch. Unfortunately for her... and me, Annie was hot on my tail walking through the door and threw her stark naked behind into the hallway so quickly she didn't even have time to cover herself up. I got knuckles that night from every man backstage; my loss was their gain.

I'm laughing at the memory when Annie opens the door and waves whoever's on the other side to come in. "Hey, Luke. I'm Quinn, Walker's fiancé."

Standing up to meet her halfway, I take her hand and give it a light kiss on top. "Well darlin, you're definitely an upgrade from the last one he was with, that lady was a nut job." I wink. "It's so nice to meet you, Walker is one lucky bastard to have snagged you."

Her cheeks blush, "He told me to watch out for your smooth lines and southern accent. He also wanted me to remind you to be on your best behavior." She shoots me a wink back. I like this one, from her strawberry blonde hair, toned body, and piercing green eyes; he's found himself a keeper. She is definitely something, but all she's doing to me right now is reminding me of those ocean blue eyes that are hopefully waiting for me out in the bar.

"Come on over and have a seat." Laughing, I wave her to the couch on the other side of the room, "Did you come all this way alone?"

"Oh, no, my girlfriends are here. They took off to the ladies' room after your set and then back to the bar to grab another drink. I'm driving tonight so I stopped after one, but those two are both a hot mess. Hopefully they make their way back here and don't agree to go home with anyone before I can get back to them. Halee claims she is on a guyatus, but when she gets a few drinks in her, there's no telling where she'll end up."

I let out a loud laugh, "What in the actual fuck is a 'guyatus'?"

She smiles, "You know, like a hiatus, but from guys."

Just then there is another knock on the door before it swings open and standing there is the woman in the yellow sweater. I blink a couple of times, shocked that Annie really went out into the bar and found her for me. "Hey princess, give me about ten more minutes and I'm all yours."

Her eyes widen, obviously confused, she looks at Quinn, then back to me, only to turn her gaze back to the woman she seems to know sitting next to me. "Um… Luke this is my friend Halee. Halee this is Luke."

Our eyes connect again and I find myself getting lost in the wave like orbs that are staring back at me.

Chapter 5

Halee

Did he just call me princess?

I swear I heard that, I mean I've probably had more to drink than I intended to but I definitely just heard this guy call me princess. I've had that nickname for most of my life, but that's what happens when you are the baby of the family with two older brothers. Then once my best friend heard it, she decided to jump on the bandwagon dragging all of our other close friends along for the ride.

I really don't mind, most of the time, but something about this sexy as sin, arrogant stranger calling me a pet name really seems to piss me off. Probably because the way he said it, like that's what he calls anyone with two legs and a vagina.

And the way he winked at me. Don't get me wrong, I'm pretty sure my insides are still doing back flips from it, but that was the cockiest wink I have ever seen. Like I'm some guaranteed prize he gets to take home for the night.

I shoot him a glare and direct my attention to my best friend, "You about ready to get out of here? If not, there's a group of guys back at the bar who offered to buy the next round." I point my thumb back in the direction I came from waiting for a reply.

Quinn goes to say something but is interrupted, "I could have one of the bartenders bring some drinks back here, princess." The two of us make eye contact and Luke squints a little like he's willing me to stay with his eyes that can't seem to make up their mind on which color they want to be.

For the first time since I entered the room, I'm really taking him all in. He no longer has his ball cap on and his unruly light brown locks look like he just ran his fingers through it. His eyes are grey in the middle but almost look like they have hues of green and blue around the rim. Luke Taylor is stunning, and judging by the look on his gorgeous face, he knows it. Breaking me out of my foggy trance he repeats himself, "What do you say princess, stay and have a drink with me?"

I examine his face and glance back over to Quinn who just smirks and raises her eyebrows at me, I've never wanted a superpower more in my life then I do right this minute. Is that a 'hell ya girl, go for it' look or is she saying 'run Hales, this boy is trouble'? I'm supposed to be on a guyatus, but damn this man looks like a god, a sex god, and my body is craving him.

I stand a little taller, "Yea sure, I'll have a drink with you, under one condition...." his self-assured look falls slightly.

"Name it."

"Don't fucking call me princess."

Quinn lets out a small snicker, stands up and extends her hand to Luke. "It was great meeting you, Walker and I would love it if you could play at our wedding. I believe your manager already cleared the date so we are all good there, and I'll call to work out the rest of the details soon." She looks between the two of us and gives her mischievous, up to something Quinn smile. "Good luck with this one, she's a spitfire."

Walking across the room towards me she leans into my ear and whispers, "You can start your guyatus tomorrow, right?" Winking, she continues out the door but stops before turning the corner, "You got thirty minutes and this party bus is heading back home, better use your time wisely."

I'm pretty sure I had to pick my jaw up off the floor to turn back around to Luke, who's just standing there with a smug look on his face. His perfect freaking face, with his day old stubble that I so desperately want... no, need to feel between my legs.

"I like her, I like her a lot. Straight to the point, no bullshit type of woman. You want that drink now prin-" he stops himself. "Halee." That's the first time he has said my name and I'm pretty sure he sang it. The way that it rolled off of those perfect lips makes me feel things that I don't want to feel.

"Yea sure, I'll take a beer please." I pause and continue looking around the room realizing what I'm doing. "You know what, a shot of tequila too, please." He gives me that sexy lopsided grin, nods his head and steps outside into the hallway to talk to one of the security guards then walks back, closing the door behind him.

We're alone. And not only are we alone but he's walking towards me with that smile. Not that half one he just gave me to tell me he approved of my drink order, this is the smile he gave me when he was up on the stage. When he made me feel like I was the only person in the room. *Pull yourself together Halee, this smile isn't just for you, I'm sure he gives it to every woman that he has had a drink with in his private room.*

Talking has never been a problem for me, but right now, staring at this sexier than sin man who is now less than an arms length away… my words are failing me. He's so close I can smell him, he smells a little like sweat and rain. I wonder what body wash he uses?

"Has anyone ever told you that your eyes remind them of the ocean?" his sultry southern voice pulls me out of the rabbit hole I was slowly falling into. My eyes find his and I slowly shake my head no, still not able to find the right words. "How about how gorgeous you are in this oversized sweater and those ridiculous looking sandals?" Once again I silently answer by shaking my head. "Or has anyone mentioned that your ass looks perfect in these shorts and the entire time I was on stage I was imagining what you look like naked."

I clear my throat, "N-no, can't say that anyone has told me those things. However, one of the guys at the bar did tell me that my clothes would look a lot better on his floor tonight and that I would sound really great screaming his name later."

Luke's jaw tightens at my words, he looks over towards the door and then back at me. "One of the assholes out there said those things to you?" He jerks his head in the direction of the bar.

"Yea, don't worry, I threw my drink on him." I give him my best wink and smirk, which causes him to bust up laughing.

"You mean to tell me that there's some asswipe out there who's soaking wet because you threw your drink on him?" I confirm with a nod which just adds fire to his belly laughing. "You Princess, are trouble with a capital T." He leans forward, runs his hands along my cheek and then tucks a strand of hair that fell forward behind my ear. Just as he started leaning into kiss me, someone came storming through the door.

"Seriously, Luke!" She yells. Oh god, this is probably his girlfriend or worse- wife, and I'm just the homewrecker that was just about to makeout with and do god knows what else with a taken man.

I glance down at his left hand as I start to back away and he grabs my waist bringing me closer. It's like he could read my mind because without looking away from me he says, "Halee, this is Annie. My manager and sister, and apparently she doesn't know how to knock."

I look over to the door, fully aware that Lukes eyes are still on me. The slim brunette is standing there with her hand on her hip looking extremely annoyed and also holding a tray with two beers and two shots on it. "Luke, first of all, I went out to find this girl for you and you already had her back here. And two, I'm not your personal drink getter, if you want something from the bar then you take your lazy ass out there and get it yourself."

He smiles at me and looks over to his sister, "Thanks, Annie. Have I ever told ya that you're the best sister I've ever had?" He reaches for the drinks, handing me my shot and beer, then gives Annie his shot while taking a long swig of his beer.

"I'm your only sister, Luke, don't try and suck up to me. This shot is apology enough, but you need to get your crap around because we have to head out."

Just then Quinn and Charlie round the corner, "We actually need to be getting home too Hales, it's getting late and JR isn't answering his phone anymore so Charlie is worried. I told her that he probably just fell asleep, but she isn't hearing it." I look at Charlie and her eyes are permanently glued to her phone, I'm sure she has sent JR about a hundred threatening text messages.

Luke leans in closer and whispers in my ear, "Come back to my hotel with me." I turn and look into his eyes, they almost seem like they're pleading with me to agree with his request. "Please. I'm not ready for this night to end, are you?" He must have sensed my hesitation because he quickly follows up with, "We don't even have to do anything, I just enjoy talking to you. What do you say?"

I take a step back, trying to escape the scent of him that has my mind agreeing to go with this man that I just met. "I'm supposed to be on a guyatis. I'm sorry, but I really should go back with them." Those words taste so bad coming out of my mouth. I don't want to go back to Iron City tonight, I want to explore everything that Luke Taylor has to offer. And once I'm done, I want to start at the top and explore him all over again.

He repeats his plea again, "Please Halee. Trust me, I don't normally do this either, but something with you feels different. I felt it the moment our eyes met when I was on stage." His pinky finger finds my pinky finger and gives it a slight squeeze. "Come on darlin', one night, what's the worst that can happen?"

"Quinn, you can head home without me. I think I'm going to hang out with Luke a little while longer." I only break our intense stare down to gaze down at his smile, this smile with his perfect dimple will be the death of me.

For a short moment I forgot that anyone else was in the room, until Quinn clears her throat. "Um, Hales. How are you going to get home?"

Before I can even think to respond, Luke looks in the direction of our audience and says, "I've got her. We're off tomorrow so my whole day is free, I'll bring her home. Maybe I can even swing over and see Walker while I'm in town, I reckon he probably misses me."

Quinn laughs, "Well we're having our monthly friends dinner tomorrow, maybe you could come to that? Don't worry about bringing anything, Princess there can fill you in on the time and place." She gives me a sweet smile that tells me to have fun but be safe, grabs ahold of Charlie's arm and heads out the door. "See you guys tomorrow, don't do anything I wouldn't do."

And just like that they're all gone, even Annie. She walked out after shaking her head and giving Luke the stink eye like she doesn't agree with his weekend plans, at all. I'm not really sure what I'm getting myself into, but judging by the way my body is reacting, I really hope that we do more than talk tonight.

Chapter 6

Luke

Sexual tension, that's the best way to describe the next hour of my life. I quickly cleaned up all my shit, said my goodbyes to anyone that was important and busted ass outta there. But the whole damn time she just looked at me with those fuck me eyes, all while biting her damn lip. What is it about a woman biting her lip that is such a turn on? No idea, but right now, Halee has me wound like a clock, and I'm about to be on her like white on rice as soon as I get this damn room key to work.

She giggles behind me. "You ok up there? You seem a little worked up for someone who just wanted to talk."

Finally the green lights flash and I push the hotel room door open, pulling her in behind me. As soon as the door is closed, I have her body pinned up against it, both arms on either side of her head, lips just mere inches from each other. "The way you've been looking at me for the past hour, I think you want to do way more than chat. And I'm feelin' that. There are plenty of things I can do to you with my mouth that has nothing to do with talking." She inhales. "You want that princess? You want my mouth on you? Sucking on your nipples which are probably hard enough to cut glass right now. Or between your legs, licking and sucking on your clit that I'm sure is currently pulsating to match the rhythm of your heart. Is it darlin? Are you wet for me right now? "

She doesn't say anything, but she doesn't have to, I can tell by the way that her chest is rising and falling to match her rapid breathing. That damn lip has found its way back in between her teeth and the fire in her eyes tells me everything I need to know.

But she doesn't leave room for assuming, "Luke, I want you and your mouth, everywhere on my body- now. We can talk afterwards."

I lift her into my arms and she immediately wraps her toned legs around my waist. Our mouths find each other, small kisses at first but when I make my way into her mouth with my tongue, I smile, she tastes like peppermint.

I can feel the warmth of her core on my stomach and it just adds to the need to be inside her. This would be the time that I typically tell the others that I'm not looking for anything serious and that after this is all said and done they'll need to leave. I don't do sleepovers, I haven't slept in the same bed as a woman since my ex.

But I don't want to tell Halee that, I can't tell her that anyways, even if I wanted to. I said that I would take her home tomorrow.

Something about her feels different, safe. So instead of going through my normal spiel, I walk her over to the bed and gently lay her down. Her Jesus sandals fall off somewhere along the way and she is making quick work of removing her shirt, bra and shorts. When she's laying there in nothing but her lacy black thong I stop her, "Let me take that off."

Reaching behind my head I pull at the collar of my shirt, tossing is across the room, then quickly I kick off my boots, dropping my pants and briefs. She lets out a gasp and when I return my eyes to hers, seeing she is focused on my dick. "Oh god Luke, I think we might need to ease into this."

Laughing, I bend down and start kissing my way up her leg, starting at her foot. "Don't worry darlin', I'll be gentle." Her back arches as I near her apex. While removing her panties with my teeth, I make small little nibbles along the inside of her thigh on the way down. Once they hit the floor, I start with light kisses around the perimeter of her mound, then I attack her clit with my tongue, while slowly inserting one finger and then two inside of her. She is tight, so tight, I'm definitely going to need to work her up a little before I enter her.

Halee lets out soft moans, her back arching off of the bed and her hands find their way to my hair and start to pull a little. "Yeah Luke, that's perfect. Oh my, that feels so good." Before she can get anything else out her legs tense up and her soaked walls are clenching around my fingers.

Damn. I wish I was inside of her right now.

After coming down from her intense orgasm, she leans up on her elbows, looking me straight in the eyes. I didn't think it was possible for her to be any more beautiful but this right here, the way her blonde hair is flipped over to one side, looking fully fucked. This is perfection at its finest. She gives me a playful grin and winks, "Thanks for that."

"Oh darlin' that was nothing. You think that was good, just wait until my cock is buried deep inside you while you come around it."

"Well, what are you waiting for cowboy, wrap that thing up and let's go." She grabs my dick and starts stroking it while I fumble for my pants to pull out the condom that I keep in my wallet. In less than a minute my shaft is covered, I make my way up the bed, appreciating her perfect tits and pink nipples along the way.

Softly I take her bottom lip in between my teeth. She makes that moaning sound again that drives me crazy and before another second passes I am sliding into the tightest pussy I think I've ever felt. I wasn't lying when I said this girl was trouble, and for some reason the entire time we make love, I can't keep that feeling I felt earlier from creeping back into my mind.

She feels like home.

Chapter 7

Halee

Holy crap. Is that what sex was always supposed to feel like? Because that, right there, was everything.

In the past, I sometimes wouldn't even get off once, but this man made magic happen twice. Luke took his time, each thrust was gentle, all while he nibbled on my neck and collarbone, and rotating his fingers between each of my breasts giving them equal amount of attention. What just happened between us wasn't just a hookup, this man I met less than three hours ago, just made love to me in a way that I've only experienced through those dirty books Charlie insists I read.

I watch him walk back towards me after discarding the condom in the bathroom trash. Luke

Taylor is beautiful. From his strong jaw that is slightly covered in day old stubble, to his perfect abs that when you follow them down lead you to a slight V on his hip bones, and if you continue south you will find the largest penis I've ever seen. I'm seriously surprised that he didn't split me in half when he glided inside me.

Luke lays back down on the bed, and props his head on his hand, "So tell me something about you Halee, other then the fact that you don't love to be called princess." He reaches over and brushes a piece of hair out of my face, then tucks it behind my ear. Suddenly I'm reminded of the events that just took place, realizing I probably look like a hot mess right now. And once again, as if he could read me like an open book he grabs my hand, "You're gorgeous darlin', I just wanted to be able to admire your whole face. Now tell me something personal, something that not many people know."

Looking up at the ceiling, I tap my finger on my lips, "Hmmm… something not many people know. Well my middle name is Sue, last name Thomas."

"Halee Sue Thomas." He reaches his hand back over to mine and shakes it, "It's really great to meet you. And although I'm glad that I know your full name now, I doubt that is your best kept secret. Come on princess, tell me something good."

"Oh no, if we are playing this game, then fair is fair. You're up rockstar… tell me something about you. What's your best kept secret?"

He runs his hand through his perfectly messy hair, " Ok, well if we're being fair, I reckon that you should probably know my full name is Luke Joseph Taylor." I have only known this man for a few hours but the way that his southern accent slips out every once in awhile, melts me.

"Just Luke or is that short for Lucas?"

"Naw darlin', just Luke." His hand finds mine again, and he starts rubbing circles around the inside of my palm with his index finger. I've never felt so completely comfortable laying naked with someone before, almost like this is normal for us. "You're up."

"I'm a hairstylist, Quinn and I own a salon in Iron City. Sometimes I feel like the luckiest girl in the world that I get to live my life, working my dream job with my best friend by my side."

That sexy lopsided grin returns, "For some reason I'm picturing you in an apron right now." I shoot him a confused look, "Oh, did I forget to mention that you aren't wearing anything else?"

I slap him on the shoulder, "You're such a man. Ok, since I already know what you do for a living, tell me something else, like how long have you been performing? Did you always know that this is what you wanted to do? Do your parents ever come with you to your gigs? Has your sister always been your manager?"

"Whoa, that was like four questions which seems a bit unfair since the only thing I know about you now is your name and occupation. But I'll bite, I've been performing since I was old enough to hold a guitar and put on mini concerts in my pop's living room. Yes, this has always been my dream, but I never imagined that it would ever become a reality. My mom isn't in the picture, she decided having a family wasn't her thing when I was young. And yeah, Annie has always been my manager, big sister, substitute mom, sounding board and basically my best friend. We fight a lot but I'm not sure either of us would have made it through life without each other. Ya know?" His eyes stayed focus on the ceiling the entire time he spoke, and when he was done he draws his attention back to me. "You close with your family? Siblings? Parents?"

"I'm sorry Luke, I might not know you very well yet, but from what I can see you seem like a decent guy. Your mom really missed out by choosing to not be involved in your life." He smiles, but I can tell that this isn't a topic that he wants to dive much deeper into right now, so I move on. "Family is everything to me, I'm the youngest of three. My two older brothers basically acted like the royal guard when it came to my dating life growing up. And if they weren't around to vet the guys I brought home then my dad was pretty efficient at it. My parents are still married, and crazy in love, it actually makes me a little sick to watch the two of them. Also, I don't mind being called princess, in fact, it's what everyone who knows me refers to me as."

Luke pulls me into his arms, wrapping my tiny body into his broad chest and rests his chin on top of my head. "I feel like I've known you my whole life princess."

We lay there, silently in the dark, just holding each other like we've been doing this for years. Once his breathing slows and I realize that he has fallen asleep, I quietly whisper "Me too" and I let myself drift off while enjoying being blissfully happy living in the moment.

Chapter 8

Luke

Just over two years. That's how long it's been since I've woken up next to a woman. The scary thing is that I'm not trippin' balls right now.

Looking over at the occupied pillow next to me I long to see her blue eyes, but the sight of her curled up alongside me, peacefully sleeping, doesn't make me sad at all. Her long, almost white hair is fanned out across the fabric, with some pieces hanging in her face. It's taken everything in me not to reach out and push them away.

But as much as I want her awake, I'm terrified of what happens next. I don't do relationships anymore, I don't do over nights, I don't do emotions- I learned my lesson a long time ago.

But I still find myself lying here next to this incredible, beautiful woman and shockingly I want it all with her.

She isn't like the others, and she's definitely nothing like my ex. Halee seems so real and down to earth, she's the girl next door and what you see is what you get.

"You're staring at me Luke, it's kind of creepy." Her eyes haven't even opened once, how in the hell did she know that I've been looking at her for easily the past thirty minutes. Before I can think of an excuse she opens her ocean like eyes and says, "Peach rings."

"Huh?"

"Peach rings. Last night when we kissed for the first time, I tasted peach rings, which I thought was odd. You were drinking beer at the club, and I never saw you put any gum in, but you still tasted so sweet."

Leaning forward I place a light kiss on her forehead, "I've wanted to do that since I woke up, but I didn't want to wake you. And the short version of why I tasted like peach rings is because I had a drink before I went on stage that is basically that candy, in a liquid version."

She lifts her hand up and runs her fingers through my untamed hair. "Will you please tell me the long version of that story?"

I pull her hand down and feather kisses along the inside of her wrist, down to her palm, and onto each of her fingertips. "You princess, are trouble and I have a feeling I would tell you anything you asked me." She smiles, pulls her bottom lip between her teeth and gives me a look that will most definitely end me. "I suppose it's not that long of a story, but when I had my first paying gig, I'd just turned twenty one. Like I said last night, Annie has always been there, my dad comes when my shows are closer to home but other than that he doesn't wander to far out. That night I was a ball of nerves, I almost didn't end up going out on stage. It was a local bar back home in Georgia, the house was packed, and I was the main act. When I was about to let my nerves get the best of me, Annie walked over, slapped me on the back of the head and handed me her drink, basically saying 'drink up'. I chugged it down in one giant gulp, then took a deep breath and walked my ass out onto that stage and killed the show. My nerves don't get like that anymore, but I still down one of those terrible whiskey drinks before every show, it's basically a tradition at this point."

Her hand found its way back to the base of my neck and is now rubbing circles, "It's so great that you and Annie have each other and I might need to try one of these famous whiskey drinks- I love peach rings."

I let out a laugh, "I think I can arrange that. Maybe next time you come to one of my shows we can drink it together."

What the hell am I implying? That this is going to become a regular thing? She was very adamant that she was taking a break from the whole dating scene and I'm not currently looking for anything serious. The only thing I planned on taking serious is my music career… that's until I saw these blue eyes standing in front of the stage last night. I knew at that moment I wanted this woman to be a part of something bigger than a one night stand.

Halee lets out a nervous giggle and as if she was reading my mind she says, "Slow down rockstar, we agreed one night. And if I remember correctly it was a pretty good night."

"Just pretty good?" I bring my hand to my chest and give her my best hurt face. "Darlin' you're going to bruise my ego."

She shrugs, "Well maybe you could remind me?" Her hand disappears under the sheet, finding its way down to my semi erect cock. A few more strokes the way she's going and it'll be standing tall in no time.

While pulling her up and on top of me I remember that I only had one condom with me.

"Shit."

Halee pulls her attention from my chest where she was licking and kissing every ab, "Uh ... that didn't sound like a good 'shit'?"

I rub my hand down my face, frustrated as hell, "So remember when I said that I don't typically do this." She gives me a confused look and sits up, giving me a better look at her perfectly tan tits and puckered pink nipples. God she isn't making this easy on me, "I don't do over nights Halee. Normally, if I pick up a girl, we do whatever it is that we intend to do and I send her home in a cab. So I only have one condom on me at a time, sadly I've used that as an excuse in the past to get them out of here. But right now I'm kicking myself because I want you so bad it hurts."

Chapter 9

Halee

He looks at me with those eyes, they're a different color this morning than they were last night, more blue tones. What he doesn't know is that we don't need a condom, but am I really willing to have unprotected sex with this guy that I just met last night? A musician at that, and if he's anything like the stereotype then he gets more ass than a toilet seat.

But I want this so bad. My inner devil and angel are having a intense battle between right and wrong and if I'm being honest with myself, If having sex with this god of a man without wrapping up his perfect penis is wrong, I want to be wrong. He reaches forward and pulls my lip that I didn't even know I was biting out of my mouth. "Princess, we can do other things, or I can run to the store quick and get some more."

I let out a sigh, "It's not that, it's just…" I feel my lip finding its way back between my teeth, it's a nervous habit. Most women probably do it to be sexy, nope, not me. "We technically don't need a condom. I… I mean, I can't get pregnant. I've just never NOT used a condom."

"Is this your way of telling me that you are on the pill?"

"No, not exactly." Crap, this is not a conversation I typically have on the first date, or ever, depending on whether or not I foresee there being a second or third date.

"Well… are you fixin' to tell me what it is exactly or should I just start guessing?"

His southern accent makes me smile, and before I have time to realize what I am doing I spit out, "I can't have kids Luke, like ever, I found out when I was seventeen. This is normally a conversation that I have at a way later date, when someone and I are discussing long-term and commitment. I don't go around having unprotected sex with random men, just because my female organs are broken."

I'm now sitting up next to him, with the sheet covering everything below my shoulders, suddenly feeling vulnerable and exposed. "Sorry I didn't mean to ruin the mood. It's just, I'm clean, and if you're clean, then there isn't anything else that we need to worry about."

I can see that there is a battle being fought inside of him, if only I could be inside his gorgeous head to hear what he is thinking right now.

"Halee…" He pauses and waits for what seems like minutes, making it obvious that he's also struggling with what's right and wrong. "Will you tell me about it?"

Everything in me wants to say no, that this is something personal that even my closest friends don't know. I don't want people looking at me with those pity eyes that I'm getting right now from the man sitting in front of me. Other than my parents, brothers and Quinn, this is a secret that I've kept hidden. A secret that I'll someday have to share with the love of my life and hope that he'll still want to be with me even though I'm physically broken and can't naturally give him a child. But as I look into Luke's eyes, I know that I can trust him, and for some reason I want to trust him with this part of me.

I clear my throat, "Well, almost ten years ago, I was at the movies with my mom and Quinn. We were watching Twilight." I laugh, remembering how obsessed I was with those books and then movies. "We were about halfway through and I suddenly felt like I was going to be sick, so I excused myself and ran to the bathroom. I won't scare you with the gory details but I ended up in the ER that night because between the throwing up and abdominal pain, it all became too much. My mom and dad refused to leave until the doctors agreed to run every test on me and figured out what was wrong."

I start to tear up, remembering the pain, not only that I was feeling but the pain in my family's eyes as we waited for the results. "Sorry, this was so long ago. I don't even know why I am crying, clearly I'm ok."

"Darlin', don't ever apologize to me or anyone else for feeling things." My hands are wrapped in his, while his thumbs lightly massage the inside of my wrists.

"After hours of testing they ended up finding a mass, about the size of a large grapefruit in my stomach. It had basically eaten my left ovary and caused tremendous damage to everything else around it, including part of my right fallopian tube. After they went in and removed it," I pull the sheet back to reveal the scar that now takes up residence across my lower abdomen. "they seemed hopeful that I might be able to conceive on my own but after running what seemed like a million other tests, they realized that the damage was just too much.

"In order for me to have a biological child I would have to go through in vitro." I take another deep breath and blink through the tears, finding his eyes again. "So, you see, condoms aren't really a necessity for me. I just don't tell most men that because I still choose to have protected sex, the last thing I need is for my vagina lips to fall off because I caught some incurable disease or something."

His chest slightly moves along with his low chuckle, "Well, your doctor did a great job on that scar because somehow I completely missed it last night while worshiping your body. And rest assured princess, I will not give you anything that will make either pair of your lips fall off. I'm actually quite fond of them and everything else about you, since we are being honest." He pulls me close to him, his lips finding the perfect place on top of my head. "Thank you for sharing that with me, I know it probably isn't easy reliving that over and over again."

"It's not, but something about you makes me feel comfortable. Almost like everything hard in life would be a hell of a lot easier with you by my side."

The words that come out of my mouth shock me, but they are true. Something about this man, with his crazy bedhead, blue-gray eyes and sexy southern accent makes me want to jump head first into whatever this is that we are doing. Even if that means I will only end up hurt in the end.

Chapter 10

Luke

Two hours, a shower and about four more rounds of sex, and we're now heading south towards Iron City. Annie looked at me like I grew two heads when I went to her room to let her know that I would be back late tonight- I was going to have dinner with Halee and her friends. After giving me the "Luke, be careful talk" she finally let me leave and meet Halee down in the lobby.

Once I got down there, the bellboy was standing a little closer than I felt comfortable with. I know that she isn't mine, but I already feel this need to claim her like she is. As I made my way towards them, I could hear Halee politely making small talk with the guy, but it's what comes next makes me puff my chest out and release my inner caveman.

When I get closer I hear him say, "So if you're in town for the night maybe we could meet up for drinks when I'm done working. The hotel has a bar, we wouldn't even have to leave."

I make my presence known as I wrap my arm around her shoulders, pulling her in close for an overly dominant kiss. Returning my gaze to him, "Think yer ah barkin' up the wrong tree there fella. I suppose you should head on over yonder and grab my truck." I hand him the valet ticket that was in my pocket.

The poor schmucks eyes get big, "I'm sorry Mr. Taylor, I didn't realize she was with you. Th-that was a great show you put on last night; me and a bunch of my buddies were there."

"Glad you enjoyed it, now how about my truck?" Still slightly annoyed that he was just hitting on my girl, then it strikes me, she isn't my girl. But damn, I want her to be. My gaze finds its way back to Halee, just as she rolls her eyes and looks away.

Which brings us to now, driving south on highway one-thirty-one, music up, windows down, her sexy ass feet on the dashboard and she won't even look in my direction. Finally, I decide that twenty minutes should be enough of a cool down period, and I try to make small talk. "So who will all be there today?"

She flips her head in my direction, "Why didn't you just pee on me Luke? That probably would've gotten your point across without you having to use so many words."

I chuckle. Yep she's pissed and that's cool, I kinda like fired up Halee. Deciding to rile her up a little more, "I mean, peeing on people isn't typically my thing, but I'm down to try almost anything at least once."

Her eyes shift to looking back out the window, apparently she didn't find my joke funny. "Hey." She doesn't budge on looking at me, so I pull over to the side of the road. Once in park, I lean over, and gently pull her chin in my direction, "Halee I'm sorry if I upset you. In the spirit of being honest, I don't really know what came over me. Seeing that guy talking to you, then hearing him proposition you like that, it set me off."

"He asked me to have a drink with him Luke." she sighs.

"He asked you to have a drink with him in a hotel bar, then followed it up with suggesting you guys didn't even have to leave. Regardless, I shouldn't have acted like that, but something about you makes me want to claim you as mine to the world. I want everyone to know that you're *with* me, and I can't even begin to explain it because I myself don't even understand it."

She clears her throat, and once again her damn lip found its way into its happy place between her teeth. "Luke…"

"No. Don't say anything, I know that I have no right. And I know that we both went into this with the idea of one night. But I don't want just one night with you Halee, I want all of your nights. When I look into your eyes, I feel like I'm home, and like I said, I can't explain the whys. Can we just ride this out and see where it goes, maybe it's only a week, or a year but maybe it could be forever." I pause, trying to gauge her reaction to me pouring my heart out. "You feel me? Can we see where this goes princess? Please?"

Letting her gaze wander back out the window, I notice how rapidly her chest is rising and falling. She looks back at me, "Luke Taylor, this goes against everything I believe in, and dating a musician is basically at the top of my 'don't do' list. Please don't hurt me… if at any point, this isn't what you want, you have to just tell me."

I lean across the center console of the truck, smiling, my lips finding hers and once again sending rapid chills throughout my body.

What she doesn't understand is that I don't think I could ever not want this.

✂✂✂

We pull into a driveway that leads up to a house that looks much nicer than anything I've ever lived in. She jumps out of the car, heads over to the garage door and types a code into the little box causing the door to open. Inside the garage sits, a black SUV that looks like it probably costs more than my house back home.

"Um… Halee." She turns her attention back in my direction and waves me to follow her. This is where she lives? It obviously must be her parents' house, or something. I know she told me that she owns a hair salon, and I know that hair stylists make decent money if they are good at what they do. But this is more than that, this house and that car are...expensive.

"Are you going to stand there in the driveway or are you going to come inside? I just have to change, throw my hair up and put some makeup on. Then we can go. As it is, we're probably already going to be late, and Quinn hates when people are late."

I pull my weight off of the side of the truck and head in her direction, "Ok cool, are your parents home?"

She laughs, "Yea, I'm sure they are home. But they live across the lake so I couldn't say for sure."

"The lake..." But before I can ask her what lake she's talking about, I'm standing in front of a row of floor to ceiling windows that are stationed at the end of her entryway. About fifty yards from the house is a tiny little beach area, with a small dock and a speedboat.

I turn around to ask her if this is really her house, but she has disappeared. So instead I follow the long hallway that leads to the kitchen, living room and dining room. All open concept with vaulted ceilings. This house isn't over the top big, but you can definitely tell that there were no expenses spared when it came to all the details.

"You ready?" I turn to find Halee in a mint green sundress, those same ugly sandals that somehow she makes look cute and her hair is piled on top of her head with a few curls floating down around her face. Don't get me wrong, this house, and that view outside is stunning. But the woman I'm looking at now is a sight that I don't think I could ever tire of. Her excitement for life radiates off of her and just in the few hours I've known her, she makes me want to be a better version of myself.

I stalk in her direction, pulling her body flush with mine. "You darlin', are pretty as a peach." Leaning down, I bring my lips to hers and the same electric current that I felt last night when we kissed that first time, is back. "Let's get going, before I say screw it and we skip dinner all together."

When we get back into the truck, she gives brief directions on how to get to Quinn and Walker's. My curiosity gets the best of me, "Halee, is that your house? Like just YOUR house?"

I look over and see a smile creep up her face, "Yep."

Yep? That's all I get? "Ok, how about we go back to our conversation from last night and you tell me something about yourself."

Her lip looks like it could detach from the rest of her body with how hard her teeth are pulling on it. She turns her head in my direction and I can tell that she's struggling with what she wants to say next. I get ready to tell her nevermind, that we don't have to talk about it, but she speaks first.

"I kind of come from money." Her shoulder shrugs nonchalantly.

I wait for her to continue but when she doesn't I say, "Ok…"

"My grandfather started a manufacturing company in Iron City over fifty years ago, and when he passed away my father took it over. What started as a small family owned business with ten people working for them, is now one of the biggest manufacturing companies in southwest Michigan. The car that I saw you drooling over in my garage was a graduation present from my parents, but the house, that's my baby. I purchased it last year, and other than using part of my inheritance for a down payment, the rest of it falls on me."

She pulls her attention back out the window and points towards the road coming up, "Take a left here, they're the third house on the right. You can see the pool off to the side and I'm sure there will be a couple of extra trucks and cars there."

When we pull into the driveway I turn the truck off and look towards Halee. She takes her seatbelt off and lets out a long sigh. "I grew up in this town and my family basically owns most of it. And not to sound ungrateful because I'm one hundred percent not. I know that I had everything I'd ever wanted, and I was able to travel to some of the most incredible places while doing amazing things because of my family's money. But when it came to making friends, I struggled with knowing who was genuine and who was just around to take in all the perks of being a *Thomas*." She uses air quotes when saying her last name. "The people that you're about to meet right now, they didn't care about how much money my family has. They've been by my side since we were in elementary school, zero questions asked. So yea, I come from money, a lot of money. The kind of money that I honestly, wouldn't have to work a day of my life. But that's not me."

I lean across the console and place a light kiss on her forehead. "Let's go meet your people."

Chapter 11

Halee

Quinn opens the door before we even make it up the steps to the porch, "It's about time. Food has been ready for at least twenty minutes. I've barely been able to keep everyone off of it." She waves us in, "Hey there, Luke, glad you could join us."

The look she's giving me right now, screams that she can't wait to get me alone so that I can tell her all the dirty details of the night. That's kind of our thing, we don't skimp out on all the sexy details. It's been that way since we were in high school, but lately she's definitely had a lot more to say in that department than I have.

Until last night.

Images from the past twelve hours replay in my head and I feel my cheeks start to blush. Quickly, I look around to make sure that no one else notices the flash of heat that just consumed my body.

As we make our way into the kitchen, the rest of the crew are coming in off of the back porch to greet us. Everyone's here this time, which seems odd considering most monthly dinners are missing a couple people due to other obligations.

Walker is the first to make his way over, shaking Luke's hand, he pulls him into one of those "bro hugs" that men do. "Luke Taylor! How long has it been man? Over a year at least, right?"

"Yea, ever since you left the windy city to come here and live the simple life." Luke looks at me, then his eyes find their way back to Walker. "However, if I'd known that the women over here in the mitten state looked like this, I probably would've jumped ship too and followed your sorry ass here."

I feel the blood rush to my cheeks and they start to heat up again. Quinn then grabs my arm to tug me in the direction of the dining room. "Come on. Help me set the table."

"You ladies need help with anything?" Luke asks.

Walker slaps him on the shoulder while letting out a laugh, "Man, the table has been set for over an hour. That's just their excuse to walk away from us so they can chat in private about you." His laugh gets even louder, "Hope you don't mind Quinn knowing just about everything there is to know, because those two have zero boundaries when it comes to their lives. Especially when talking about bedroom activities."

Quinn and I have rounded the corner to the other room where Charlie is waiting. No wonder everyone is here today, they all want to know what happened with me and the sexy musician last night. Our group is so close, that there aren't many secrets that don't eventually make their way to everyone. It's like that old game we used to play when we were children, the telephone game. It starts out with facts, but by the time it gets to the last person in line, there's a sliver of truth left, and the rest of the story has been completely exaggerated. So who knows what story they've all heard by now.

Quinn and Charlie are both staring and waiting on me to start to spill the details that I'd also want to know if I was on the other side of this interrogation. When I don't just dump it on them, Charlie chimes in, "Sooo…. What happened last night?"

For the third time since I walked through the door of this house. I feel my face start to heat, the images from the night before begin to flash through my mind. "Well I mean, what didn't happen would probably be a better question."

The two of them squeal and Quinn pushes for more, "I knew it! Tell us everything."

"Well for starters, did you guys know that it is physically possible to have multiple orgasms in one night? Because I didn't. Hell, some of the guys that I've been with didn't even deliver one, let alone seven."

"Seven!!!" Charlie shouts, and quickly covers her mouth when she realizes how loud she was. "Seven... you're exaggerating right? I mean, that's a lot. How are you even walking, talking, or being a functioning human right now?"

Charlie turns and silently mouths 'Seven' to Quinn who is carrying a smug look on her face. "Walker and I's record is six in one day, but I see this as a challenge to beat your record. Game on sister- Game. Fucking. On."

"Seven." Charlie whispers again under her breath. "Holy cow. So what's next for you and the sexy southern sex god?"

I cover my face with my hands, "Ugh, I don't know."

Quinn pulls my hands from my face, lifting my chin up so we are looking eye to eye. "Did you guys talk about what comes next? Is there more or was last night simply a booty call and he's just driving you here out of obligation because he said he would?"

"No, I don't think it's that. You guys should've seen him this morning. He went to talk to his sister and tell her what was going on and by the time he made it down to the lobby, I was getting hit on by another guy. I'm not kidding when I say that he all but peed on me to get the point across to this poor guy that I'm not available. And when we were on the way here, he pulled over to the side of the road, and asked me to see where this goes with him."

Quinn being the best friend that she is, senses the sadness in my voice. "So why do I get the feeling that you're questioning and second guessing all of this?"

I throw my hands in the air, "Oh I don't know, maybe because he's a super sexy musician who is constantly on the road, having other incredibly attractive, half dressed women throwing themselves at him. He even admitted that he's the king of one night stands. And lets not forget that I'm on a guyatus." Or at least I was supposed to be. "The last thing I need to do right now is get into a relationship with someone who lives in a completely different state the majority of the time, and could have a different woman every night if he wanted to." I let out a long sigh, "No, thank you."

Quinn and Charlie both open their mouths to say something, but Walker comes around the corner and luckily interrupts whatever speech they were about to give. "You ladies done gossiping yet? Because we're all starving."

✄<✄<✄

Dinner seemed to go about like normal, other than the third degree that JR insisted on giving Luke. And even though Walker has known Luke for a lot longer than he's known me, I sensed some hesitation in even his words throughout the evening. But for the most part, he fit in and got along with my friends like they were his own. Which makes the jumbled thoughts inside my head even harder to try and unscramble. This man checks off just about every box in my mental checklist and something about him makes me feel like I can truly trust him. Not only have I agreed to unprotected sex with this man that I barely know, but I opened up to him about my past health issues, and then I told him about my insecurities from growing up in a family that has money. Something about Luke has me forgetting when I should stop talking, and even though Quinn says this is a good thing, I don't know if I agree. This scares the crap out of me, everything about him should have me running in the other direction.

So why is it that I'm sitting in the passenger seat of his truck, on the way to my house. Why didn't I just take JR up on his offer to drop me off on his way home? Why did I agree to let Luke bring me, when he all but pleaded with his eyes, that decided they wanted to be more of a golden brown shade tonight.

I can't answer all the questions as to why. All I know is that I'm not ready for him to leave. What happens when he drives away and there's a possibility that I might never see him again. I know earlier he said that he wanted to see where this can go, but what if it only goes until Thursday night when he has another show, and another woman captivates him while he's on stage.

"If you keep biting that lip Halee, you're likely to pierce a hole straight through it." His deep voice brings me back to the present and I look over and give him an encouraging smile. "Penny for your thoughts?"

I start shaking my head, and I can feel my lip make its way back in between my teeth. "What are we doing Luke? What is this?" I motion with my fingers back and forth between us. "I have to be honest with you. I'm a hopeless romantic, and on paper you're perfect for me in just about every way. The fact that you have known me for less than twenty four hours and you've already picked up on little things that most men don't in months. But we don't even live in the same state as each other, and this is where my life is. I can't just pick up and move… not that you're asking me to. But I'm twenty-eight years old, and at this point in my life I need to start thinking about my future. And not to sound brash but having a fuck buddy that lives in Chicago isn't exactly part of the plan."

After we pull into my driveway, he turns the truck off, lifts the center console and pulls me over to him so my legs are draped across his lap. He grabs my hands and locks his eyes on mine like he means business. "Darlin', I don't want to be your 'fuck buddy'. I mean don't get me wrong, I definitely want to fuck you. I want to strip you down until your body is fully exposed, lay you across your bed and kiss every part of you until you are moaning my name. Just like you did last night." I squeeze my thighs together slightly, hoping he doesn't notice the effect his words are having on me.

"But Halee that's not all that I want." He reaches his hand out and pulls my lip from between my teeth.

"What do you want Luke?" My voice trembles.

"I want all of you."

"How could you possibly know that already? Just this morning you were admitting to me that you're a one night stand kind of guy, that you don't sleep with them more than once, and you definitely don't let them stay overnight. So why me Luke? Why am I different?"

He smiles so big I swear that his cheeks are going to collide with his eyes, and that sexy dimple that seems to make me fall even harder, appears. "I don't know princess. I don't know what makes you different and if I'm being real, I've been asking myself the same question all damn day. But with you, I find myself wanting to break all the rules that I made after…"

He stops, and suddenly that smile that was just radiating across his face, falls. "After what Luke? Why are you like this? Why don't you let

anyone beside Annie and your dad in anymore?"
His head shakes back in forth and I can see the
internal struggle that is happening behind his eyes.

"Come on, Luke. Tell me your secrets."

Chapter 12

Luke

"Come on Luke, tell me your secrets."

I want to tell her everything.

Why I don't let people in so easily. I want to tell her how the last time I did, the person I gave myself to shattered every part of me. I want to tell her that up until I saw her last night, I was just a husk of a man and that somehow, she makes me want to open up and be whole again.

But I can't tell her any of that. At least not yet, "That secret is for another day. But I will tell you… Halee Sue Thomas, something about you makes me feel like home. When I look into your mesmerizing blue eyes, it's like I'm looking into the ocean back in Georgia. All I want to do is sit down and write songs for the world to hear about how incredible you make me feel. I know that we've only known each other for a short time, but I almost feel as if I've known you my entire life."

Once again, that full, pouty lip has found its way back to the hold that her teeth seem to have on it. I can see that her mind is in overdrive trying to process the words that are coming out of my mouth. If this was one of those cartoons that Annie and I used to watch when we were younger she would definitely have smoke coming out of her ears.

"Halee, I know the miles between where we live is going to be hard. And I'm not asking you to marry me, but what I am asking is that you give us a fair shot. Because it terrifies me to think that if we don't, we'll always wonder what if." I pull her the rest of the way onto my lap so she's straddling me. "Give us a shot darlin', and I promise that I'll drag my sorry ass back to Iron City every chance I get."

Her lips come crashing down on mine so fiercely that I don't need to stop and ask for her answer. She's saying everything that I need her to say, right now, with her intense kisses. My hands work their way under her dress and up to cup her boobs, while her fingers wiggle their way from the back of my neck, up, through my hair.

She's grinding on me and I can feel the heat of her core through my shorts, so I know she can feel the growth that's happening underneath her.

We grind and dry hump each other, all while our mouths never part; until we hear a light tapping on the passenger side window. I'm not sure how long this has been going on for but the windows are completely covered in steam.

I turn the truck key over and roll the window down so we can see who is on the other side.

"Oh, Mrs. Blakey. How are you doing tonight?" Halee shifts off of my lap so that she's sitting on the seat next to me. I'm trying my hardest to conceal the massive erection that's currently taking up space in my shorts.

"It's a lovely night dear, but I must say, you and your *friend* there are putting on quite the performance for the rest of the neighborhood. Might I suggest you take that display, inside, where other people can't see you." The elderly woman's eyes reach around Halee and find me. I give her my best 'Luke Taylor smile', I mean why not, it works on every other person with female genitalia. "By all means, please continue with your *friend*, but maybe in the privacy of your own home."

She gives us a devilish wink and turns to head back to her house. "You got it Mrs. Blakey." Halee shouts as I roll the window back up. We look at each other for a few seconds before we both break into laughter.

"Come on *friend,* lets go inside so you can finish what you started. My panties seem to be a little more wet than what they were before you kissed me into next week."

Lord, this woman will be the end of me.

✂✂✂

Halee rolls off the top of me, both of our bodies are slick with sweat as we try to calm down our erotic breathing. "Damn, I'm pretty sure my heart might have stopped there at the end. That was intense, darlin'."

"That. Was. Amazing." She says in between sharp breaths, "I honestly thought last night and this morning was just like a fluke thing and that the sex wouldn't always be that great. But that was incredible Luke. That thing you did with your tongue on my clit… if you could just do that every day for the rest of my life, I would be a happy woman."

I let out a laugh, "You got it, princess. But does that mean I get to spend the rest of my life with you?"

Her body freezes.

Damnit, why do I have to keep bringing up the future instead of just living in the moment with this woman? "I'm just joking Halee, don't freak out on me here." When she lets out a deep exhale I ask, "I know I have my reasons for not wanting to jump into a serious relationship, but what has you so freaked out?"

I use her own words on her, "Tell me your secrets, Darlin'."

Halee rolls to her side and props her head up on her hand, "If I told you, I would have to kill you."

"Come on, Halee. I'll tell you, if you tell me." I raise my eyebrows, trying to entice her in my offer knowing that I hate talking about my last relationship with anyone. But it's worth it if it means that she will open up to me, even a little.

"Well then, in that case, how can I say no to you." Her lip creeps its way into its happy place and I can tell that she is thinking carefully about what she wants to tell me. "I've had shit luck when it comes to dating. I already told you that when I was growing up I had a hard time knowing who was genuine and who was just using me for my family's extravagant lifestyle. My parents definitely tried to keep me, Graham and Will grounded and not let the money go to our heads. But that doesn't mean that they also didn't spoil the crap out of us and our friends. Most of high school was made up of heartbreak after heartbreak, and after that it just continued."

I reach over and stroke her cheek with my thumb, "That doesn't make any sense, you're the most beautiful, fun, witty and intelligent woman I've ever met. Any man would be lucky to have you."

"And in my early twenties, they definitely wanted me, and I'm embarrassed to admit that quite a few of them got me. But apparently I'm just the girl you have a good time with before you find the woman that you spend forever with. Lately most of the guys I meet don't make it to a second or third date because it is obvious they aren't looking for anything serious.

"That's why I'm so hesitant to throw myself into whatever it is we are doing, Luke. Again, you seem like a great guy. You're ambitious, talented, you seem to have a great head on your shoulders, you get along with my friends, and you definitely aren't terrible to look at." She runs her fingers from the day old stubble on my chin all the way down to my abs. "You are the definition of danger for me. I can see myself falling for you, heck, I feel like I'm already falling for you. And if you break me, I don't know if I'll be able to recover from it."

I pull her into my arms, and she lays her head on my chest, "Darlin', the last thing I want to do is hurt you. Trust me, I'm just as hesitant about this as you are. But like I said, this, with us, feels different. Jump into this with me princess- we owe it to ourselves to figure out what we can be."

Chapter 13

Luke

"Do you have to leave tonight? I really wouldn't mind doing this all night." Halee is curled up into my side, her head and palm resting on my bare chest.

I'm not even sure what time it is, after we both agreed to give this thing between us a real shot, we celebrated with another hot round of sex. This time, instead of her being on top, I took complete control and manipulated her body into every position I could think of.

The way her body responds to my touches could keep me hard for days. One light kiss along her collarbone and her nipples harden instantly.

She starts to draw shapes on my abs with her finger and it brings me back to the present. "I could probably stay the night, I'll just have to get up super early and head back to get Annie and the rest of our equipment. But the early start will be worth it if I get to snuggle your sexy ass all night."

I feel her shoulders relax, "I would love that. As long as you don't mind the early start."

"Darlin' I would go without sleep if it meant extra time with you. I probably won't be able to get back here for a couple of weeks. Annie has scheduled back to back gigs starting this Thursday through the following weekend."

"That sister of yours is a slave driver. Should you text her and let her know that you're staying here tonight, so she doesn't worry about you."

"Naw, I don't really feel like dealing with her throwing a hissy fit. Then tonight will just go to hell in a handbasket because she's so damn relentless."

She turns her head up so she's looking me in the eyes, her fingers still roaming around my chest and abdomen. "Should I be concerned that she hates me or is she like this with all women?"

I laugh, "Basically all women after what happened with my last relationship. It probably doesn't help that we met at one of my shows, she basically thinks everyone I meet is just a groupie that's trying to get their shot at fame."

"Does this have anything to do with the secret that you've been putting off since I told you mine? You can tell me anything Luke."

"Ok, but I'm warning you, it's quite the story…"

"I guess it's a good thing we have all night then, huh, rockstar?"

The show that I was scheduled to do tonight was cancelled due to a busted pipe so I get to surprise my girl. I have been working my ass off trying to get bigger gigs lately which means we haven't really gotten to see each other much. But this weekend I'm all hers and what she doesn't know is that I plan on finally making the leap and proposing. I've had the ring for a couple of months but I just haven't felt like it was ever the right time.

But this weekend will be our one year anniversary and even though Annie seems to think that this is way to soon, I have to disagree. Kam is who I want to spend the rest of my life with, without a doubt. She's always so understanding and supportive when it comes to my music, never one to bitch or complain about my late hours. It's like she was made for me and this industry, and I don't plan on letting her get away.

As I pull into the driveway I notice the cars of her two best friends are there. She told me earlier that she was having the girls over for a movie and wine night. Hopefully they don't mind me crashing or even better, they'll take the hint and leave so we can have some alone time. When I walk into the side door I hear music and laughing, they sound like they've already hit it heavy with the wine.

I sneak in and close the door softly, trying my best to be quiet so I can scare the shit out of them. Before I can reach the living room, I hear Kam talking but it's what she is saying that seems to stop me in my tracks.

"No, typically he isn't the type of guy I'd be with, but Luke Taylor is going to be famous someday. Just wait and see, and I want to be onboard for that ride."

One of her friends laughs and says, "Well at least he isn't terrible to look at. I mean if I had to stay with someone who I wasn't all that interested in, I'd hope he'd look like Luke."

"I know, I know." Kam says, "He definitely is nice on the eyes. But I just always saw myself

being with a athlete- musicians are always so broody and sensitive. He always wants to talk about his feelings or tell me how I make him feel."

Her other friend lets out a dramatic sigh, "Do you hear yourself right now Kam? You're sitting here complaining about this sexy as hell man, who wants to tell you how much you mean to him all the time and who loves you. Boy, you sure have it rough."

"Guys, I'm not saying Luke isn't a great guy. He just honestly isn't the guy for me." I can feel my blood starting to boil. What in the actual fuck have we been doing together for the past year? She approached me, she said she loved me first. Kam is the one who wanted all of this to progress the way it has.

"So, why stay with him?" One of her friends asks the million dollar question. I listen closely for her answer, knowing that when I asked her this later, she probably wouldn't have been as honest as she is being right now.

"Because he's going to blow up soon. You girls have heard him, he's going to be huge. And I want to be Mrs. Luke Taylor when he makes it big. If in a few years we 'drift' apart and get a divorce, then so be it. But by then I'll have at least one or two children with him. I'll collect child support, my

name will be out there and I will eventually be able to snag another big name."

The way she speaks, it's like she is proud to be a gold digging tramp. At this point, all I'm seeing is red, my whole body is shaking, completely unaware that my feet started to move in the direction of the living room.

"Get the fuck out of my house!" I scream. All three heads flip in my direction and their faces have guilt written all over them. "I don't think I stuttered… Get. The. Fuck. Out. Of. My. House. NOW!"

"Luke, baby! What are you doing home. And that's no way to speak to my friends, I invited them over here."

I charge past her in the direction of our bedroom, stopping at the closet in the hallway to grab her suitcase. "I wasn't talking about your friends, Kam. I'm talking about you! They at least are decent human beings who realize that trying to trap a man into a loveless marriage by getting pregnant is crazy."

I start throwing her clothes into the open suitcase, but she takes them out just as quickly. She has tears flowing down her cheeks but they are probably just as fake as this relationship is. "Luke, don't do this. Please! I don't know what you *heard but I can explain. You can't just throw me out, I moved to Chicago with you. I don't have anywhere to go."*

"That's not my problem, sweetheart. I reckon you should've thought about all of that beforehand. Get out Kam, before I start throwing your shit out the front door."

I head to the kitchen and grab a beer, while she stomps her spoiled ass around the house collecting all of her things. At some point, her friends thought it was a good idea to leave. I can't say that I blame them, I would leave right now too if I could. But damn it, this is my house and I ain't going to just run away with my tail between my legs. I'm Luke Fucking Taylor, and I will be damned if I let another woman into my life who just wants to hitch a ride to fame.

"Oh my god, Luke, that's terrible. Did you ever hear from her again after that night?"

I look back into the baby blue eyes that are looking up at me, reminding myself that Halee isn't Kam. "Yea, she tried saying a few weeks later that she was pregnant and that it was mine. But turned out it was just her grasping at straws. There was no baby and I had never been more relieved. I can't imagine being tied to her sort of crazy for the rest of my life."

Halee sits up, pulling the sheet to cover her chest, "Do you want kids Luke? I mean, you know that I can't have kids naturally, so, you don't have to worry about me trying to trap you. But if we're thinking about seeing where this goes, I want to make sure that you really understand and are ok with it."

I pull her so she is back laying next to me, and kiss her on her forehead. "Don't worry princess, I understand. And to answer your questions, yeah, someday I think I would love a couple of youngins running around, but not for a few years. I really want to focus on my career and right now, babies would just complicate things that I don't need complicated." I pull her chin up and take her bottom lip into my mouth, giving it a break from the strong hold between her teeth. "And if in a few years, you and I are still together and we want kids… we will figure it out. Sound good?"

"Sounds perfect."

Chapter 14

Halee

The light shining through the curtains wakes me up from an intense dream I was living in. A dream where I was making love to an exceptionally sexy musician who knew how to give me multiple orgasms within minutes of each other. Oh wait, that wasn't a dream, that is real life...

The side of the bed where he slept is cold but the pillow still smells like him. Even though he warned me that he would have to leave before dawn, it doesn't stop the ping of disappointment that I feel when I don't wake to his perfect face this morning.

Replacing him is a folded up piece of paper lying on the bedside table. I make my way across his side of the bed, but stop my thoughts as I realize how crazy I sound. Calling it his side of the bed when he has only slept in it once and we have only known each other for a couple of days.

I wasn't exaggerating when I said that I could see myself falling for him and fast. He's everything I could've ever wanted in a man and now my stomach lives in a constant state of butterflies when he is around. From the flirty looks, to the subtle touches as he walks by me, and the way that he seems to have already picked up on the small mannerisms that most men never do. Luke Taylor is perfect for me. So why am I left with this nagging feeling in the pit of me, telling me that this will end in nothing but pain and heartbreak?

Everything inside me is telling me to pull away. I can't get hurt if I remove myself before we get in too deep.

I open up the folded paper.

Good Morning Princess,
I wanted nothing more than to wake you up this morning
so I could see those beautiful blue eyes that remind me of
home. But I figured since I kept you up all night with all
of our sexapades, that I should let you sleep.

Halee Sue Thomas, I'm not sure what you are doing to me
but I've never wanted to not leave someone as much as
I do right now. I'll be counting down the hours until I
get to see your gorgeous face again. Don't question this

darlin'.

Yours- Luke

And just like that, all the fear of the unknowns drift away from me. How did he know that I would wake up this morning and start to question everything that has happened. Am I really capable of being with a man who basically every night has to get up on stage in front of hundreds of women? Women who want him just like I wanted him two nights ago at his show. Women who probably also get wet just from his sexy wink or his panty soaking smile.

Trust has never been something that came easy for me. But I know now, after reading that note, that I have to give this... us, a fair chance. I have to put myself out there, knowing damn well I could get hurt in the process.

It's Monday, so that means sushi and shopping with my best girl. I make my way to the bathroom- as much as I hate the idea of washing Luke off of me, I smell like sex. And Quinn will already be asking enough questions as it is, she doesn't need any added ammunition.

✂<✂<✂

"So have you heard from him at all today? I mean obviously other than the incredibly sweet love note he left on your pillow?" Quinn says while shoving her favorite California roll into her mouth.

Guilt washes over me, "No. I haven't texted him because I don't really know how this works. Yeah, we exchanged phone numbers and yeah, we maybe had mind blowing sex all weekend. But what if now that he's back into his everyday routine he's realized that he doesn't really want to be tied down to someone who lives in Iron City, Michigan." I throw the balled up straw wrapper across the table at her, "And he didn't leave it on my pillow, he left it on the nightstand."

"Ok Hales, but maybe we should be a little less concerned with *where* he left it, and zero in on the fact that this man left you a love note. And if I read it correctly, he's asking you to not overthink this. Which is exactly what you're doing. Text the man."

She's right, I push the little, annoying voice in the back of my head that's saying 'maybe he doesn't want someone like me' to the side. I pull my phone out of my purse and a smile takes over my face, Luke's name is on the lock screen.

Luke: Tell me a secret, princess.

My heart melts as I read his words, nothing has changed. He still wants this, me, just as much as he did last night.

Me: Well you see, I had this super sexy rockstar in my bed last night. And waking up alone all but ruined me. I'm not sure how my body can become so accustomed to having you near in a mere couple of days. But the secret is out… I miss you Luke Taylor.

I see the little three dot bubble appear and then disappear again. Oh god, did I say too much? He's probably running for the hills and changing his identity now thinking he has a stage five clinger on his hands. I set my phone down and try to make light conversation with Quinn, asking her about wedding stuff.

"I still can't believe your wedding is only eight months away. You deserve…" my phone lighting up immediately halts my words.

Luke: Darlin' those words are exactly what I needed to hear from you. When you didn't text me this morning I was worried that you were shitin' bricks about us. You're all I can think about. I can't wait to see you again.

"Earth to Halee, I deserve...?" Quinn pulls me back to our conversation and I decided to shoot Luke one last text telling him that I'm at lunch with Quinn and will call him later.

"Sorry. And as much as it pains me to say this... you were right. I want to give this thing with Luke a real try. But what I was saying is, you deserve all the happiness in the world Quinn. I'm so glad that you and Walker found each other, and I feel so lucky to stand up with you guys at your wedding."

A small tear slips down onto her cheek and she quickly brushes it away, "After Brett, I never thought I could feel this way about a man again. But knowing Walker, and feeling the love that radiates off of that man for me, I know that he was sent to heal me. And Hales, I want that for you. Maybe Luke is the guy who comes in and changes everything, or maybe he isn't. But don't think for one second that I'm going to let you get away with not trying. What would've happened if you wouldn't have pushed me so hard to let Walker in? It's my turn to push you. Take the leap Hales, it could end up being the best decision you've ever made."

Now my tears are cascading down my face, "I don't know how I'd do life without you Q, thanks for being my person."

She gives me her best Quinn wink; we both pull ourselves together and enjoy the rest of lunch.

Sitting across from my best friend, our favorite sushi rolls covering the table between us, making plans for her wedding day, and the feeling of hope in my heart that maybe I can be as hopelessly happy as she is one day.

This is exactly where I want to be.

Chapter 15

Luke

June

It's been a week since I've seen her face in person. We've been texting nonstop since last Monday and we have even been sneaking in some late night sexy FaceTiming when I don't have a show. But it isn't enough. I want her next to me, falling asleep in my arms at night, waking up with her messy blonde hair covering the pillow next to me.

My sister keeps saying I'm acting like a lovesick puppy but I can't help it. For the first time in years, I'm actually excited for a future with a woman. And that's saying a lot because I was sure after everything that happened with Kam, I was eternally broken.

Annie has been pretty hesitant when it comes to talking about anything that has to do with this relationship with Halee. All she keeps saying is 'be careful Luke' or 'make sure you are thinking with the right head Luke' or her favorite 'keep your eyes on the prize Luke, and I don't mean the open legs that are waiting for you back in Michigan'.

I know she's right, I need to stay focused, more now than ever. There's been a lot of talk that there have been some big names in the audience at my last few gigs. Annie keeps getting calls and emails about the possibility of big things happening. She doesn't tell me much, I think she's worried that I'll get in my head too much and somehow screw this up. So I'm taking her advice and doing what I do best, letting her handle the rest of it.

My phone in my pocket vibrates as we are setting up at a venue and preparing for sound check.

Princess: Tell me a secret, rockstar.

I love that she calls me rockstar. In the past when other women have said it, while they basically drooled over me, did nothing but turn me off. But when she says it, I know it's just payback for always calling her princess.

Me: I'm setting up for a gig tonight. Don't get me wrong, I'm just as pumped as any other night, I just wish that when I got on that stage tonight and the lights flash out to the crowd, it was your face that I see standing front and center.

Princess: Me too, babe, me too. Want to know my secret? Last night after we got off of the phone, you had me so worked up with your words that I let my hand travel down under my panties and I orgasmed so hard while imagining it was you touching me.

Jesus Christ, I look around and make sure no one is looking at me and the obvious half chub my woman just gave me.

Me: Damn Halee, I'm standing in the middle of a club getting ready for a sound check with a hard on now because of you and that dirty mouth of yours.

Me: I have a show in northern Indiana this Saturday night. I looked it up, and I think it's only about a two hour drive from where you are. You should see if Walker and Quinn want to come, and then we can all go out afterwards. You can stay the night with me and I'll show you all the things I can do that'll have you screaming my name.

Her response takes less than thirty seconds.

Princess: YES!

Princess: Even if those two don't want to come, I'll be there. Just tell me the time and place. I miss you so much Luke and not just your talent in the bedroom... I miss all of you.

She doesn't even know that I feel the same way. In the short time that we have known each other, she has wiggled her way into my heart. Somewhere between the flirty texts throughout the day, to our deep and meaningful talks at night, I think I've fallen deep for this girl.

Me: Same darlin'. But I would feel a lot better if you didn't go down there alone. I won't be able to keep much of an eye on you until the show is over.

Me: I gotta go princess, it's time for sound check and Annie looks like she might actually explode if I don't get my ass out there.

Princess: Later rockstar. *Kiss face emoji*

✂✂✂

The rest of the week surprisingly went by in a blur. I've had three shows so far, and tonight will make four. The two days that I wasn't playing a show, I was basically holed up in my room writing new songs. Something about Halee has me feeling extra inspired these days.

Even though Annie isn't a huge fan of this whole thing, she can't deny that I'm putting out some seriously great lyrics since meeting Halee.

"Luke, you ready?" Annie calls through the door that divides our hotel suites. Tonight is the night, I finally get to see my girl's face after twelve long-ass days. Halee texted earlier and told me that they had to wait until Walker got off shift at six and then they would head out. But she was worried that they might miss the start of the show, depending on how bad traffic was on the way down.

"Yeah sis, I'll meet you in the lobby in about five minutes, I just have to throw my shoes on." I holler back.

When we get to the venue there's already a crazy long line wrapped around the outside of the building. It's crazy to think that these people are here to see me. Lately, the fans have been out of control, but luckily this place has a rear entrance so I can sneak in unnoticed.

The mass of people reminds me, "Annie, did you remember to put Halee and the others on the VIP list so that they don't have to wait in line to get in?"

"Yes, Luke." She lets out an exaggerated eye roll.

"And did you get them the passes so they can get backstage as soon as the show is over?"

This time she lets out an actual annoyed sigh. "Yes. Luke."

"What's your problem with all of this exactly? I mean I get it, you're worried that I'm going to get my heart broke again, but she's different, Annie." I put my hand on her arm, "I appreciate you going all big sister on me and putting my ass in check whenever I've needed it, but don't you reckon that I know what I'm doing?"

We walk into my private area backstage and she shuts the door behind us. "Listen, I'm just concerned that this girl's going to come in and make you forget what's important. You've been working your whole damn life towards this and big things are happening Luke. Do you even know how many important people are going to be here tonight?" She waits for my reply but I just raise my eyebrows and shrug my shoulders in question. "At least five. There'll be at least five people out there tonight who could decide that you're the next big thing; who could change your life forever. And instead of you concentrating on killing it tonight, all you're focused on is seeing some girl that you just met three weeks ago.

"I know you think she's different Luke, but how can you know for sure. You met her the exact same way you met Kam and look how well that turned out. All I'm asking is that you stay focused on the end game. And for god sakes, make sure you are wearing a condom with this girl."

I feel my blood start to boil, "Dammit Annie! She is different. And you would know that if you'd even give her the time of day. Plus, not that it's any of your fucking business but Halee can't even have kids naturally, so if you think she's just in this to try and trap me, you're barkin' up the wrong tree."

She throws her hands up in surrender, "Look, I'm sorry. I don't want to fight with you, especially twenty minutes before you're going to go on stage. I'm going to go get our whiskey drinks and I will be back. This show's important, don't screw it up by not having your head in the game."

I look at my phone when she walks out of the room and see that I have a text from Halee.

Princess: Knock 'em dead rockstar... If you have any issues with stage fright, just picture me naked. *wink face emoji*

Instant relief takes over my just foul mood. How can Annie not see that this amazing woman just makes me a happier version of myself. If she thinks that my head isn't all the way in this, she's wrong. I can have my dream of playing on the big stage someday to sold out arenas. I *will* have my dream, but I will also have Halee. That much I am sure of.

Chapter 16

Halee

Luke's show is a madhouse. If I thought the last venue I saw him play at was huge, you could fit three of those clubs inside this one. There are two levels and both are completely covered in women who are dressed in clothes that barely cover the essential parts. The skinny jeans, strappy heels and baby blue off the shoulder shirt I'm wearing makes me feel extremely over dressed in comparison to these other women. I guess the difference is that they're trying to gain his attention, and I already have it.

The idea of Luke possibly being a big time music star hasn't really hit me until this moment- I'm seeing these women fawn over my incredibly sexy man on the stage in front of us. In between songs you hear some of them scream out crazy things like 'I love you, Luke' or 'Luke, please have my babies'.

I'm pretty sure that one of the women all the way up front just took her panties off and threw them up on stage at him. "Oh my god, Hales, did that crazy lady just take her underwear off and fling them at him?"

I swallow as I try to remember that he's up on that stage to not only put on a good show but to also draw people in. He once told me that the idea is to leave the fans wanting more. And the way he keeps flashing around his 'panty soaking smile' with that perfect freaking dimple, has my stomach in knots.

As if Walker could sense the uneasiness that has consumed my body. He comes around the other side of Quinn and wraps his arm around my shoulders, pulling me into a brother bear side-hug. "This is all a show Hales, remember that. At the end of the night he's going home with you, not any of them. Don't tear yourself up by overthinking everything."

A wave of nausea hits, and I find myself quickly needing to locate the closest bathroom. "I'll be right back guys, I think I just need a minute." I shout to them over the lyrics I've come to memorize, that are being perfectly played behind me.

When I make it to the bathroom, surprisingly it's empty. I guess no one wants to miss the sexy performance of the one and only *Luke Taylor*. I lean over the sink and look at myself in the mirror. What am I even thinking, I can't even do this week after week, let alone possibly year after year. All of these women in here tonight want him, and most of them are just as pretty, if not prettier than I am. "This is all too much." I say out loud just as the bathroom door opens up.

Quinn walks up and wraps her arms around me from behind, laying her cheek on the top of my head. Even with my heels on, she's still taller than I am. "What's going on in that head of yours?"

"You didn't have to follow me in here ya know, I would have been just fine." I turn around so we're facing each other.

"I know that, and honestly, I was going to leave you to sort out your thoughts alone. But you see, my fiancé out there… you have become like a sister to him. And as much as he likes Luke, he loves you Hales, we both do, and he insisted that I come make sure you're ok. Now why don't you tell me what is going on in that pretty little blonde head of yours."

I throw my arms in the air and let out an exhausted breath, "This is all just so much, Q. I mean yeah, the last time we came to his show, women were just as mesmerized by him as they are now. And yeah they were all half dressed and flaunting all of their assets, just like they are tonight. But I don't know, it feels different this time."

"Because now he's yours and you've never really been great at sharing?" She gives me a sympathetic smile.

I return her smile with my own, "I hate sharing." My smile fades, "And what happens when someone else in the front row of one of these shows grabs his attention and he decides that he wants them instead? Quinn, I think I'm falling in love with him. Hell, I think I fell in love with him that day he came to your house and fit in so well with all of us."

"Oh sweetie, have you told him this?"

"What? Have I told him that after three weeks that I think I'm head over heels, crazy in love with him? No, that has not come up in our late night conversations. It's crazy right? There's no way that I can already be in love with him. Right?"

"I don't think it's all that crazy Hales, I'm pretty sure that I fell in love with Walker the day he helped me move all of Brett's stuff out and took it to the shelter. And that was only after a couple weeks of knowing him." The look of sympathy still shadows her face, "Let's head back out there before we miss your man's entire show. But listen, if I have any advice for you it's don't fight what you are feeling. At the end of the day, the heart wants what it wants and the longer you fight it, it's just more time you could be spending together."

By the end of the show, I have a decent buzz on and my shirt is damp from sweat from dancing. I figured if you can't beat 'em, you might as well join 'em. So in between songs I screamed out how sexy he was and I swayed my hips along to the many songs that I knew he had just written about me.

We make our way backstage and the minute his dressing room door is open I'm on him before he can even turn around to see who walked in. He turns so we're face to face and wraps his arms around my waist, lifting me off the ground. "I have missed you so much, Luke."

His lips meet mine and that jolt of electricity that I've been missing returns. How is it possible that I was just thinking about walking away from this man and the way he makes me feel.

He lowers me down to the ground and cups my face in his giant hands, bringing our foreheads together. "Darlin', you are a sight for sore eyes."

Someone clears their throat from across the room and it reminds me that I wasn't the only one that walked into this room moments ago. But instead of Walker or Quinn, who are just standing there smiling, Annie is the one responsible for the interrupting noise. "Luke, we have about forty five minutes to tear down and get out of here. I suggest you get a move on it."

I know that she isn't my biggest fan but the fact that she doesn't even acknowledge me does nothing but aggravate me. So in true Halee Thomas fashion I go out of my way to kill her with kindness, "Hey Annie, it's great to see you again. Do you want to join the four of us for a late dinner and drinks? After Luke helps pack up, of course."

"Hello Halee. And no, thank you. There's still business to tend to tonight. Just because the show is over doesn't mean we all get to stop working." She glares at Luke and leaves the room.

"Your sister hates me."

He pulls me into another embrace and kisses the tip of my nose. "Naw, she's just worried about me. I'm sure she will come around eventually."

✄✄✄

"Holy shit princess. I think you outdid yourself that time. Whatever you were doing with your hips while arching your back, it was amazing." I roll off the top of him and curl up into his side.

After the show, we ended up at a great pub down the road that was dimly lit so that between Luke wearing a ball cap and the lights being low, no one recognized it was him.

We ate, drank and laughed as the four of us exchanged stories from our lives before we all met. Luke and Walker told tales of when they would go out in Chicago and the kind of trouble they seemed to get into. Quinn and I shared stories about when we were kids, or our high school years, the men seemed to be overly fascinated by the fact that we were both cheerleaders. If I read my best friend and her fiancé right, I'd guess that she still pulls that uniform out now and again for a little role play.

When we were done at the pub we parted ways, Luke and I jumped into a cab and headed back to the hotel he's staying at. And the other two decided to make the trip home since Walker didn't have anything to drink all night.

We barely made it into our room before we were ripping each others clothes off and throwing them as we worked our way to the bed. Luke had me riding out my first orgasm with his mouth within seconds, and before I had even come down, he buried himself deep inside of me.

"Tell me a secret, Halee."

I pull my body up the side of his so that we are now face to face, "My body feels empty when you aren't inside of me." My cheeks blush at what I'm about to admit to him. "I think you've ruined me for all other men because I've never felt the way that I do right now."

He brushes the loose hair out of my face and tucks it behind my ear. "That's perfect princess, because I don't want to share you with any other man. I want to be the only person who gets to experience that ungodly good feeling of entering you." Trailing his hand down my body he cups my apex, "This is mine, and only mine. You good with that?"

I swallow and shake my head up and down. The sudden need to confess my feelings from earlier tonight takes over me, "I almost walked away tonight Luke."

His hand leaves my core and he tilts my chin back up to meet his blazing eyes. "What does that mean Halee, walked away from what?"

"From this, us." I point back and forth as I sit up, grabbing his shirt off the end of the bed and putting it on. If we are going to have a serious conversation I need to at least put my tits away. "Seeing all of those women throw themselves at you like they did tonight, it triggered my biggest fear. What if I'm not enough for you Luke? You're going to be this big, famous rockstar and blow up stages with your raw sexiness and talent. What if one day you decide that you don't want to be with someone like me?"

He's now also sitting up and leaning against the headboard, "Darlin' that's a lot of 'what ifs'. I want you, all of you. Damn it Halee, I think I'm in love with you and I know that's fucking nuts but it's true. You're the light I see at the end of the tunnel, you're the person I see sharing all the fame and success with. You're the woman that I see keeping me grounded and my head on my shoulders when the big things finally do happen. I want you, all of you, please don't ever question that. I may smile, or wink back at those women when I'm on stage but it's nothing but a performance princess. You're who

I'm singing about when I'm up there spilling my heart out to the world. It's you, I want it to always be you, Halee Thomas. Please don't give up on me. On us. I know that this'll be tough, but I promise it'll be worth it."

He may have kept talking, but I didn't hear anything else he said after he told me that he loved me. "Say something Halee, I'm a basket of nerves over here."

"I love you, too, Luke." I pull his shirt back off of me and climb onto his lap so I'm straddling his already growing erection. "I think I've loved you from the second I saw you."

"Well, butter my butt and call me a biscuit!"

I giggle. "I'm not sure what that even means, but you sure are cute when you talk all southern like that." I bring my mouth to his neck and pepper kisses along his jawline. "Tell me a secret."

His breathing is shallow, as he tries to hide the way his body is reacting to my light nibbles on his earlobes. "What do you want to know?"

"Tell me your biggest fear. I just told you that mine is not being enough. Tell me yours."

Our foreheads are together, noses just millimeters away from each other, and as I look into his hazel eyes I see nothing but honesty. "My biggest fear is that I'll be able to see my dream right in front of me but somehow not be able to reach it. I've been working my entire life for what comes next and I think that would ruin me."

"Not going to happen rockstar… all of your dreams are going to come true."

Chapter 17

Halee

August

Three months.

That's how long Luke and I have been doing this long distance thing. We talk and FaceTime as much as possible and when we aren't doing that we're sharing secrets through our texts. Most of the time the secret I share isn't much of a secret at all, nine times out of ten I reply with 'I miss you so much it hurts'. And that's the honest to god truth.

I try to make it to as many of his shows that are close, and he tries to come here any chance he can get away for a couple days. I'm pretty sure that Annie hates me even more now than she did in the beginning, except now she likes to claim that I'm nothing but a distraction.

Luke's constantly reminding me that she's only looking out for him and that she'll eventually realize that I'm the best person for him. But I'm not sure how long it takes for someone to completely change their outlook on you. In her eyes, all I am is just some groupie he met at a show, and although to an outsider it may look pretty accurate, it's the furthest from the truth. I want big things for him, and not because I want to be known as Mrs. Luke Taylor. I want this for him because I know how badly he wants it, and how hard he has worked for it.

I wouldn't dream of stepping in the way of his dream. Which is why, even though this distance has physically been making me sick, I deal with it.

For the past three weeks, my stomach has been in knots. I keep saying it's just my body's reaction to the other half of me not being around.

"Jesus, Charlie, what did you bring for lunch today? The entire salon smells." I walk back into the breakroom after cashing out my client out.

"It's chicken and broccoli casserole. What's up with you lately? I feel like every smell has been bothering you?" Charlie set her bowl down and crossed her arms over her chest. "Just last week you complained all day about how our color line must have reformulated because the smell was so much stronger. But Quinn and I don't think it smells any different than normal."

I pull my salad out of the mini fridge we keep in the back for snacks, lunches and bottled water. "You guys are crazy, the smell is so much stronger once it's oxidized than it used to be. And as far as your lunch, that broccoli smells like dirty socks."

"What are we talking about?" Quinn walks in the back room and starts rinsing out color bowls.

"We're talking about how sensitive Halee's nose has been these past couple weeks." Charlie shoots me a glare and goes back to eating her gym sock casserole.

Quinn turns around, wiping her hands on the towel, and leans up against the counter. "Not just your nose is sensitive Hales, you started crying the other day when that adopt a pet commercial was on the TV here too. And your mood swings are out of control."

Charlie laughs.

"What the hell is so funny?" It's now my turn to shoot daggers out of my eyes at her.

"Oh nothing. It's just that, if I didn't know any better I'd say that you're pregnant. These are all the same symptoms I had when Tucker was growing inside of me."

"Well that IS funny considering I was told that I can NEVER have kids. So... I guess we can just chalk it all up to me being a nut job." I close the lid on my salad and put it back in the fridge. Lately I struggle to find anything that tastes good, and when I do finally find something, I devour all of it.

I mean to a normal person, it definitely does sound like pregnancy craziness but I'm not normal. Just crazy.

"Hales, when's the last time you had your period?" Quinn is looking at me with that mom look she gets when the conversation is going to get serious.

"Guys! What part of 'We are so sorry to tell you this Halee but you will unfortunately never be able to conceive children naturally' don't the two of you understand?"

Quinn rolls her eyes, "Your period, Halee, when was your last one?"

"Ugh, I don't know. Last month, maybe the month before. I haven't really been regular since they removed my one ovary so I honestly don't keep track anymore."

Thinking back to last month, I think I remember Aunt Flow paying her annoying visit but I really couldn't say for sure. But why does any of this even matter? These two seem to be ignoring the big picture here, and that is, whatever is left of my female organs are not in working order anymore.

Charlie starts to take her apron off and grabs her car keys out of her cabinet. "Where the hell are you going? Don't you have like five more clients today?"

"I do, but I have twenty minutes before my next one gets here so I'm going to run to the drug store and buy your stubborn ass a pregnancy test. I'll be back in ten."

I roll my eyes and just as I'm about to walk out of the back room to go find something else to do to get me away from Quinns patronizing stare, my phone screen lights up with Luke's name.

Luke: Tell me a secret.

Me: I work with a couple of crazy people. And I miss you. What's your secret rockstar?

Luke: *crying laughing emoji* You love working with those two, and you live for their crazy. I miss you too darlin'.

Me: You're right, but I think they've really lost their marbles today. Waiting impatiently for your secret...

Luke: Ok ok... You don't have to miss me for too much longer. I'll be in your bed tonight.

Me: Luke Taylor, don't you dare make jokes about me seeing your ruggedly handsome face.

Luke: Not joking one bit princess. But it will be late so don't feel like you have to wait up. I'll use my key and just sneak into bed whenever I get there.

Me: How long do I get you for?

Luke: Forever

Me: Haha, but seriously. When do you have to head back to Chicago or to the next gig.

Luke: Two days.

Me: It'll never be long enough, but I will take what I can get. See you tonight Rockstar. I love you.

Luke: I love you more, princess.

Me: Not possible *wink face*

✄<✄<✄

I finally had a break long enough to go to pee and before I could even make it through the door of the bathroom, Charlie is shoving the pink box that has two pregnancy test inside into my hands.

"Just pee on both of them. You know, just in case one of them is faulty."

I give her a sideways look and take the box from her hands. "This is so ridiculous, and by the way, I am not paying you for this. I told you it was a waste of money."

"Well maybe you're right, but you know what… doctors are wrong everyday. They also told my dad that he would never have kids, and here I am, a goddamn miracle standing right in front of you. Take the tests, Halee. Then we'll know for sure."

I wash my hands and look at the two white sticks that I set on the back of the toilet. Who knew how hard it was to try to hit those things while peeing. Hopefully I got enough on them to work and officially get the girls off of my back.

I read the back of the box while I wait. It says they can take up to five minutes to completely read so I glance down at my watch.

Two more minutes. Then we can go back to our normal everyday activities.

Two lines?

Hmm, what did two lines mean?

I pull the white paper back out of the box and flip it until I find the instructions in English.

Two lines, two lines… I know I saw it in here. Oh, there, two lines!

Pregnant?!?

Well that can't be right. I glance at the other test. That one also has two lines on the screen.

What are the chances that Charlie bought two tests and they are both expired or faulty or something. I think to myself, probably *about the same as the chances of me getting pregnant.*

I grab the two tests and shove them into the front pocket of my apron, disposing the rest of the evidence into the bottom of the trash bin.

There has to be a better test than this one. I know I've seen them on commercials where they actually say 'pregnant' or 'not pregnant'. I just need to get one of those.

Somehow, I need to get out of here without a million freaking questions from my friends, but first, I need to call and reschedule my last two haircuts of the day.

Chapter 18

Luke

When I pull into Halee's driveway I notice that there's still lights on inside. I glance down at the clock and see that it's well after midnight and I assumed that she would be sleeping by now.

I keep my keys out just in case she left lights on knowing that I was coming and the door was still locked. But I don't need them. The knob turns easily, I drop my guitar case and bags on the floor, eager to get to my girl.

We've been really trying to make the best out of the circumstances but I can tell that it has been taking a toll on Halee. And if I'm being honest, it's driving me crazy as well. Everything about this woman has me wanting a normal, domestic and simple life. And I know that it'll never be an option, especially after what I just found out tonight.

Everything I've ever wanted as far as the dream that pertains to my career, all came true about four hours ago. As soon as I was done meeting with Annie and my new agent after my gig tonight, I hauled ass to Iron City to tell my girl that everything I've worked towards is finally happening. Next week I'll take off with one of the biggest country stars in today's music and be his opening act for the last leg of his tour. Something about the band that was opening for him is splitting up due to two of the bandmates sleeping with each other. I really didn't listen much after they told me the job was mine.

Everything I've ever wanted in life is happening and I can't imagine not having Halee by my side through it all. This may be my dream job but she is my dream girl and the few short months that we've been together has made me realize I don't want a life without her.

When I walk into the living room, I find Halee curled up at one end of the large sectional couch with her favorite blanket draped over her. She must've tried waiting up for me but judging by her closed eyes it looks like she failed.

I lean down and press a gentle kiss to her forehead. "Hey darlin'. I'm here. Why don't we go to bed."

Her body tenses and her eyes pop open. It almost looks like the rims of them are a light shade of pink, like she was crying. I remember her saying that her allergies were kicking her butt earlier this week. That must be it.

"Hey rockstar. I stayed up because I wanted to talk to you about something."

Excitement shoots through my whole body and the urge to share my news takes over. "Wait me first… Halee it's happening."

"What's happening?"

"Everything I've ever wanted. Annie and I had a meeting with an agent tonight, starting next weekend I'll fly to Dallas and join the last leg of Braden Smithton's tour. Halee, it's twelve weeks, and I want you to come with me. I already know what you're going to say, 'you can't just up and leave'. But you can. Quinn and Charlie can handle everything at the salon. My dreams are coming true, princess, everything I've worked for. It's all finally happening for me."

She just blinks a few times and her now glazed eyes are about as wide as golf balls.

"Say something Halee. What's wrong?"

She clears her throat and tries to hold herself together but I can tell that she's just seconds away from falling apart. I lean over to reach for her hand but she pulls back.

"L-Luke…" Her body begins to shake as she gives in to the sobs, "Luke, I can't be with you anymore."

What? I have to be hearing things, did she just say that she can't be with me? "What are you saying Halee?"

She stands up and starts to pace the empty floor space in front of me. Her arms are tightly wrapped around her body like she's trying to comfort herself for what she is about to say next. "I'm sorry, I thought I could do this but I can't. Especially now with you going on tour. Luke, I want this for you, more than you know, but I just can't be a part of your journey. Musician's girlfriend isn't the life that I want, all the traveling, and the women throwing themselves at you."

My stomach feels like it has made its way up into my throat, I think I'm going to be sick.

"Halee, you can't just walk away from us. I know how much you love me, I see it in your eyes when we're together. I hear it in your voice when we're apart. Don't do this darlin', please don't do this."

I stand up, making my way in her direction but she steps back and puts her hands out to keep me away. "Please Luke, don't make this any harder than it has to be. We have had a good run, good laughs, great sex, but we both knew that this probably wasn't going to last forever. Maybe we can be friends."

"Friends! Are you fucking kidding me? I don't want to be your friend Halee. Not. A. Fucking. Chance." I run my hands through my hair and pull them down my face. "What, you just want me to pretend that you aren't the love of my life. Watch you go on dates with other guys... oh I know, maybe we can double date."

"Don't be an ass, Luke."

"Me? Be an ass? Huh, that's funny. So what, was this just a game that you were playing? String the already broken rockstar along, get him to open up and make him believe that you love him as much as he loves you. Then break his heart into a million pieces?"

She opens her mouth to talk but stops. The floodgates have opened and her tears are flowing down her red cheeks. I raise my hand up, "Save it, princess. And no, sorry, I don't want to be your friend. Have a good life Halee."

I walk out of the living room, grab my shit off the hallway floor and slam the door on my way out. I may be about to live out my childhood fantasy by singing to stadiums full of fans, but I know one thing's for sure…

My heart is still inside that house.

Chapter 19

Luke

September

Me: Just finished up my first show on the tour. We're in Denver... God I miss you Halee. I miss hearing your voice, listening to you giggle, but most of all I miss your secrets.

Me: Tell me a secret princess...

Chapter 20

Luke

October

Me: It's been almost two months darlin'. I've tried giving you space but it's killing me. It's crazy how much someone can completely consume all of your thoughts, all day, every day. How are you? Do you think of me like I think of you?

Me: Tell me a secret princess…

Me: Jesus, Halee. Just say something. Anything.

Chapter 21

Luke

November

Me: What I wouldn't give to hear one of your secrets again. Please, Halee.

Me: Halee.

For the first time in months, the little bubble with three dots appears on the screen. But then it disappears just as quickly as it showed up. Why am I doing this to myself? She doesn't want me anymore. She's made that clear.

So why am I sitting here pining over someone who obviously doesn't want anything to do with me.

It's time to let go and move on.

Me: Have a good life Halee.

I turn off my phone, throw it on the bed and head off the tour bus to get ready for my show. I don't know what will happen next, but what I do know is I'm done chasing Halee Thomas.

Chapter 22

Halee

December

My life consists of a bunch of numbers these days.

Six.

The number of months I've been baking a tiny little human body inside of me. I rub my hand over the small bump that has finally decided to grace us with its presence. For the longest time I just looked like I was letting myself go. I heard all the whispers that people thought they were being discreet about. But now the word seems to be out, Halee Thomas is in fact having a baby, and rumor has it that she doesn't even know who the dad is.

The problem is, I know exactly who the dad is.

Five.

The number of months that I've gone without seeing Luke. When he slammed my front door that night, and walked away, he took everything with him. Including my heart.

I know it's my fault.

"Halee, where are you at?" I hear Quinn heading up the stairs.

"In the bathroom." I holler back. After leaving the salon, I stopped at the drugstore on the way home and bought just about every damn pregnancy test that they had on the shelves. Convincing myself that the two Charlie bought were definitely faulty and there was no way I was pregnant. But judging by the dozen of positive tests that are surrounding me, mixed in with the empty bottles of water, I am in fact 'with child'.

There's a light knock on the door before my best friend enters the room, taking in her surroundings and obviously trying to gauge the situation "Are these all positive, Hales?"

"Yep, every damn one of them. Can you believe that?" I let out an obnoxious laugh- it's either laugh or cry, and I've done enough crying over the past few hours to last me a lifetime. I bury my head in my palms, "God Q, what am I going to do?"

She sits down on the cold tile floor next to me, moving a few of the life altering sticks out of the way. "What do you mean what are you going to do? Halee, you're going to have a baby. Don't you see how magical this is?"

"Quinn, he just told me how having kids right now would do nothing but put a damper on his dreams and goals."

"Now, I'm sure that's not what was said. And even if it was, none of it will matter the minute you tell him he's going to be a daddy. That man is crazy about you, and you love him, so what if this wasn't part of the plan. You guys will make a new plan, and he will just have to adjust his dreams a little. It's all going to work out Hales, I know it." She wraps her arms around me, *providing the comfort and strength I need to mentally work through this.*

"I'm going to be a mommy." I whisper, while running my hand over my still flat belly. Everything's going to be ok, there are worse things in life than creating a small miracle child with the man you love. Hopefully that man agrees.

"You are going to be the best mommy, Hales."

When they told me I couldn't conceive naturally, I just kind of put the idea of ever having kids in a box, and put it in the back of my head. I convinced myself that I didn't want children, figuring it would be less of a disappointment down the road.

But that night, when Luke showed up and started talking about how all of his dreams were coming true. My mind flashed back to that night when he told me that his biggest fear was being able to see his dream right in front of him, only to come up short and not being able to reach it.

All I could think about the entire time he talked about the plans he already made for us in his head, was that there is no possible way a baby would fit into this equation. So as much as it hurt, and trust me it hurt, I pushed the man I love away and let him believe that I didn't want him anymore.

Eight.

The number of times he's texted me, and most of the time all they would say was 'Tell me a secret princess'. I've never replied to any of them. I know that it may seem childish or immature to just completely ignore him like I have, but I knew that the only secret that I wanted to tell him is that I'm carrying his baby.

I thought that maybe after the tour was over I would go to him and confess everything. But then Walker told me that Annie called to cancel Luke performing at the wedding because he got an offer to be the second act for another big headliner.

His dreams are coming true. And I knew that Luke being the man that he is, if he found out I was pregnant, he would give it all up to be a dad. I can't let him do that. The last thing I want is him someday resenting me or even worse, the little bean in my belly.

"Halee, are you ok?" Charlie's voice wakes me out of my dream like state. I'm staring out the window of the church that Walker and Quinn are getting married in today. Leave it to my best friend to decide to get married on New Years Eve, but her theory is that every year, people all over the world will be celebrating their anniversary with them.

"I'm perfect, just feeling Bean move around in there. It's crazy, now that I actually know it's him and not just gas." I rub my hand across the navy blue dress that flows perfectly along my growing belly. No hiding this thing now.

"Him? Did you find out what you are having?" Charlie squats in front of me, bringing both hands up to hold my bump.

"No, no. I just keep having dreams about a little boy who has perfect hazel eyes and rich brown hair just like his daddy." My voice cracks as I try to get the word daddy out. I know I'm going to have to tell him eventually, but for now, it's just me and Bean.

Charlie brings her face super close and whispers, "Hello little Bean, this is your Aunt Charlie. We all love you so much already. You and I have to stick together, you know since we are both little miracle babies."

She stands up when we hear the bathroom door open. Quinn walks through with her mom carrying the train of her perfect white mermaid style dress. Her strawberry hair is pulled to one side in loose curls, and even though she originally had a veil, Walker begged her not to wear it. He said that he wanted to see her beautiful green eyes the moment the doors opened.

We both gasp, "Quinn! You. Are. Stunning."

Charlie's head is nodding up and down, and she is trying to salvage her make up by blotting her eyes with a tissue. You would think that she was the pregnant one, not me. "I don't think I've ever seen a bride as beautiful as you."

Quinn's smile is radiating and she throws her hand on her hip, "Charlie, you were a bride once. I'm sure that you were a knockout."

Her head falls back in a large laugh that shakes her body, "Girl, I was seven months pregnant and at the courthouse wearing white capris and a blouse. Knockout isn't exactly the word I'd use to describe it. Speaking of my failed marriage though... guess who's officially divorced." She throws her arm in the air. "This girl."

"Oh, come on girls, clearly talking about failed marriages on someones wedding day can't be good juju." Quinn's mom is touching up her makeup and hair in the bathroom mirror.

"Q, I forgot to ask. Did you and Walker ever decide on what song you were going to pick for your first dance?" I swear, my best friend has binders full of wedding plans but when we were all together last weekend making the centerpieces for the reception, they admitted that they still didn't have a song picked out.

"You know what. Walker asked if he could be in charge of the song. And as much as it kills me to not know what he picked, I love the idea of it being a surprise."

The door opens, and Mr. Harris informs his daughter that it's time.

As we make our way down the aisle, I find myself surveying the crowd looking for *him.* Walker told me last week that Luke sent him a text apologizing, saying that he just couldn't make it. So I know that he isn't here, but it doesn't stop me from looking. Maybe even hoping.

When the doors open and close for the final time, Quinn and her dad walk through, and in that moment I understand. I know exactly why Walker didn't want her wearing a veil. Her emerald eyes are beaming as she walks in our direction.

I break my focus on her, and look over at her groom, who is completely hypnotized by the woman walking towards him. I find that my hand has worked its way down to Bean and I can't help thinking about how I will never have this.

And almost like my thoughts conjured him out of thin air, the large wood doors open one more time and sure as shit, Luke and some bimbo in a skin tight, Barbie pink dress walk in. The entire room turns and looks at the new guests and I take this moment to cover my stomach with the bouquet of flowers in my now trembling hands.

Chapter 23

Luke

I couldn't seem to take my eyes off of her
the entire ceremony. And other than when Tiffany,
shit, or is it Brittany? Is it sad that I can't even seem
to keep them straight these days? Besides when
my date and I walked in, she has made it a point to
not even look in my direction.

Since the day Halee ripped my heart out of
my chest and kicked me out of not just her house,
but also her life, I've been a human wrecking ball.
Annie continues to try and slow me down but she

can't, no one can. The drinking and the women seem to be the only thing that dulls the pain of living life without Halee Thomas.

She was supposed to be the one riding out this amazing dream with me, not the long legged blonde standing next to me. Or the tiny short blonde two nights ago that I insisted on only fucking from behind because in those moments, I could pretend it was the back of Halee's head as I railed her.

But it's not Halee. None of them are. And what hurts me the most is that I actually believed a woman as amazing as her would want to be with someone like me. That she would just be ok with the constant traveling and all the groupies throwing themselves at me, day in and day out. Last week, I finally sat down and started going through my fan mail that was beginning to pile up. I still can't seem to wrap my head around the fact that women think it's ok to send naked pictures of themselves. I decided to let Annie handle the fan mail from then on out.

I didn't just give up after I left that night. Although my pride told me I should. Nope, instead I reached out more times than I can count, hoping with each one it would be the day that she would finally text back. Eventually, all I would send was

'Tell me a secret.' It was me pulling at straws, and I knew that, but I was desperate.

"Hey stud, I grabbed you a beer from the bar. You ready to go find our seats?" Right when 'legs' wraps her arm through mine, my eyes find the only person in the room that matters. Except she isn't alone, there is a man standing next to her that is slightly shorter than I am but looks like he could possibly pick up a small car and throw it. To someone else he would be intimidating but the fact that his arm is casually draped around my girls shoulders has me seeing red.

Halee throws her head back in laughter at whatever the hulk just said but then something happens. Her bubbly giggles stop, her eyes go wide and her hands find their way to her stomach. As she turns to the side I notice that her once flat abdomen is now slightly rounded and it only takes me a few seconds to come to the conclusion that she's pregnant.

I stand there for what seems like minutes trying to calculate exactly how far along she must be to be showing as much as she already is. But my thought process comes to a sudden halt when I see that man whose arm was just touching her, bend down on his knee, put both hands on her belly and starts talking to the child.

My child. It has to be mine...right?

Before I can think about anything else, I'm storming in the direction of the seemingly happy couple. "What the fuck, Halee. Are you pregnant? Who's this asshole? Is he the dad?" I point towards her stomach that her hands are now wrapped around like she needs to protect what is growing inside of her. "Is that my baby Halee? God damnit, say something!!"

Chapter 24

Halee

Say something.

Say anything.

This can't happen here. Not on the most important day of Quinn and Walker's life. He wasn't supposed to be here, I was supposed to have more time to figure out what I was going to say to him. How I was going to explain that I hid this from him so that he could pursue his dreams without being held back?

The whole scene is playing out in front of me but I can't hear anything over the pounding of my heart. "Halee!" My brother Graham's voice pulls me out of whatever trance I was in. "Who the hell is this guy?"

"Who am I?" Luke laughs, "I'm most likely the father of that baby that you were just talking to, asshole. Who the fuck are you?"

Graham looks at me with wide eyes. He just came back to town after being medically discharged from the Army, and his fiancé isn't able to move until the end of the school year since she's a teacher, so he agreed to be my plus one at the wedding. Before he can say anything, I step closer to Luke. "Can we please talk about this another time, you're making a scene and this day isn't about you and me. Or him." I rub my hand over my protruding belly.

"Him?" Luke's eyes go wide, and then soften, his voice sounding a little more broken this time.

His tall, beautiful, blonde date is looking between all of us like we're doing a hard math problem and she can't seem to keep up. "Ahhh, would someone like to tell me what's going on?"

"Yea, I think that you and I have something to talk about darlin'. Unless you are telling me that that isn't my child?" Luke's eyes shoot in the direction of my brother.

Just as Graham is about to introduce himself and probably remove any questions that this is his child that I'm carrying, the DJ comes onto the microphone. "Ladies and Gentleman, please help me give a warm welcome to the new Mr. and Mrs. Walker McCoy." The room erupts into cheers as they walk in, holding hands, completely oblivious to the shit show that is happening in the corner. That's exactly how it needs to stay, the last thing they need is to be worrying about me and Luke on their wedding day. "Please clear the dance floor so the newlyweds can have their first dance."

As the song starts up, my eyes find the eyes that have been haunting my dreams for the past five months. The eyes I keep picturing our little boy that looks just like his daddy having. The eyes that are so infused with pain right now. It kills me knowing that I'm the cause behind the pain. "Please Luke, can we talk about this tomorrow? I will answer any questions you have for me. Just let's not do this here, I'm begging you."

"I can't talk tomorrow Halee, I have to be back on the road at eight in the morning. The only reason I'm here is because our show was outdoors and it got cancelled due to weather."

"Fine, tonight. After the reception. Can you come over?" My eyes pleading with his to give me the next few hours to be present in my best friend's wedding day.

"Yea, ok." He runs his hands through his hair that is now longer and even more unruly than when I last saw him. It has my mind wondering if anyone else has cut his hair since the last time I did. "I'll be at your house."

He turns, giving Graham a daring look before retreating in the direction of the doors. His date keeps trying to slow him down but he shrugs her off over and over until he is out of the door and out of sight.

I run my hands down my face and let out a long sigh. "I think I'm going to be sick or pass out. I need to sit down."

Graham ushers me over to a chair off to the side where I have the perfect view of my childhood best friend having her first dance as a married woman to the love of her life. The song that Walker picked is perfect, On My Way To You, by Cody

Johnson. The lyrics hit home so perfectly for the two of them, all the obstacles they have overcome to get to each other.

Tears begin to stream down my face as I watch Walker sing and spin Quinn around the dance floor. Her smile is so large that it might actually break her face. '*It was all worthwhile, when I finally saw you smile…*' Yep, he definitely hit it out of the ballpark with that song, it was like it was made specifically for them.

When the song ends, I know I need to make my way towards the head table and prepare for my maid of honor speech. As I stand, Graham pulls me back into the chair. "Oh no you don't little sis. Care to explain to me why that man doesn't know he's going to be a father in just a few short months? I thought you told mom and dad that the baby wasn't his and that you guys split up because he wasn't the dad?"

I cover my face with my hands, "Oh Graham, I've made a huge mess of everything. I told everyone that because I knew that if you all knew the truth, someone would tell him."

"Are you saying that he really didn't know that you are pregnant until today?"

"Yeah." Guilt and shame course through my veins, and I think Graham can see it.

"Princess." He lays his hand on my arm, while shaking his head. "I know you must have your reasons behind why you thought this was the best thing to do but you better hope he's an understanding and forgiving man. I don't know how easily I would get over someone hiding from me that I was going to be a father."

"Graham, the baby isn't even here yet. It's not like I have robbed him of time with his child."

He gives me a weak smile, "Are you saying that in the past six months you haven't spent every moment bonding and being excited about the fact that you are going to be a parent. Going to doctors appointments, seeing your baby on that black and white screen. You're saying none of that has mattered? Because in my eyes, you stole all of those moments from him the day you decided to keep this monumental secret from him."

The word secret bounces around inside of me. He has been texting me for months asking me to tell him a secret, should I have said something? I shake my head, "I can't have this talk right now Graham, I have to prepare myself for my speech. And for the record, I did this for him. I went to all of those appointments alone, for him. I endured all of those women giving me looks of sympathy that I was alone, for him. He's finally living out his dream of being a famous rockstar, and I'll be damned if me and this baby are the reason he walked away from it all."

I storm away from my older brother with anger seeping out of me. I know he's right, and I know that everyone is going to feel the exact same way as he does when they find out I lied to them all about it.

But I stand by what I did.

I did this FOR him.

Chapter 25

Halee

The drive home from the reception venue seemed to take longer than it did the night before. Last night, my thoughts were consumed with last minute things that needed to be done before the big wedding day. But tonight, all I can think about is what is going to happen when Luke gets to my house.

Graham offered to come with me, if I thought that Luke would get physical but I knew better. He's going to be angry, and he'll one hundred percent be hurt but I know for a fact that he would never lay a hand on me.

My mind trails back to my maid of honor speech…

I would like to start off by congratulating and thanking the happy couple. It's been an honor to stand by your side today, Quinn, and watch you marry the man who completes you.

The two of us have basically been inseparable since we were in kindergarten. We always said that God knew our parents couldn't handle us as sisters so he made us best friends. Quinn, you have always been my moral compass in life. Most days you're the little angel that sits on my shoulder telling me I should probably not do this. But sometimes you're the devil sitting on the other side saying, 'oh what the hell, Hales, you only live once'. I can't imagine what my life would've been like without you by my side.

And as much as it kills me to share you, I know that the man you chose to marry is the best guy for the job. He knows how to reel you in when your crazy is showing, but he also knows when you need to let your freak flag fly.

Watching you two love has been one of the greatest blessings of all time. Your love is unconditional and I hope one day I'll find someone who looks at me the way you two look at each other.

Let's all raise our glasses and celebrate the happy couple. Here's to a lifetime of making everyone else in the room uncomfortable with the way you guys are constantly undressing each other with your eyes.

I love you both... cheers, everyone.

There was a pit in my stomach after my speech as I searched the room for Luke. Part of me wonders if I had my greatest love already, but it's too late. I've really screwed this up big time, and I don't think there's any way to make it better.

As I pull into my driveway, I notice a strange truck that I assume is Luke's rental already sitting out on the side of the road. As I get closer, my thoughts are confirmed when I see the saddest vision of the man I love sitting on my front step.

After parking in the garage and gathering all my energy and courage to get out and face my problems head on, I notice Luke in my rearview. He doesn't look angry anymore, not like he did at the reception, now he just looks a little confused, but mostly hurt.

"Hey." My voice is shaky, as I step out into the cold, now January air.

"Hey."

"It's cold out here, let's go inside. I can make you some coffee or warm tea if you want."

He lets out a sigh, "Yeah… that sounds good."

Once we get inside the door, his hand finds my arm and spins me around so my back in pinned against the door. He brings his head down so that our foreheads are touching but nothing else. Even just from the small amount of contact, my body is already buzzing with need of him.

"Halee, I need you to tell me right now. Is that my baby?"

I close my eyes and take in a long breath, when I open them again, I find his hazel orbs blurred by unshed tears.

"Yes."

Luke's eyes snap shut and his hand slams the door directly to the right of my head. He backs away, and his hands find their way to his messy hair and then to the back of his neck. "Damn it Halee! Why the hell didn't you tell me."

"Please Luke, can we go and make some tea, let me change into something more comfortable. This strapless bra has been digging into my belly all night. Then we'll sit down and I'll tell you everything. Just please Luke. Give me ten minutes."

He lets out a sarcastic laugh, and throws his arms in the direction of the kitchen. "Lead the way princess. You've already kept this from me for months, I suppose I can wait another ten minutes."

My eyes begin to blur as I make my way past him towards the kitchen to do what I promised. My grandma always said that a mug of warm tea could fix just about any problem in the world, but I have a feeling she was unaware of how badly I could royally screw up when she told me that.

Chapter 26

Luke

Whose life am I living right now? Ten hours ago my biggest problem was seeing my ex at her best friend's wedding and making sure that the girl on my arm was hot enough to make her jealous.

Needless to say Legs, my date, was less than impressed when I dropped her off at the hotel room, grabbed all my shit and said I would see her around. I drove straight to Halee's and sat on her front step for hours just thinking about how in the hell this happened.

I mean, I know how it happened. Obviously. I was definitely present that day of health class when the creepy ass health teacher explained precautionary sex to us and then slowly lowered a condom onto a banana.

But how is Halee pregnant?

My mind instantly went to the idea that she lied about it all and this was nothing but a trap, that she is in fact like all the other women I've come across in my years of being in this industry.

But I know Halee, and I just can't bring myself to believe that I was that stupid to fall hopelessly in love with a scam artist.

"Want to go in the living room?" Her sweet voice startles me, I didn't even hear her come back down the stairs. I turn and take in everything that she has to offer. Her bare feet padding across the kitchen floor, the sexy black yoga pants that shows off the roundness of her perfect ass, the Iron City cheer team shirt that I've seen her wear a dozen times, but now it stretches a little tighter against her growing bump. But as my gaze wanders up to her face, I find that her lip still hides in its favorite place between her teeth. And her eyes, those ocean blue eyes, still after all these months make me feel like home.

All the anger that was entrapped in my body mere seconds ago is released as I stare at the woman who stole my heart. "Yeah, the living room is fine with me."

She sits on one end of the sectional with her legs crossed and hand resting on top of the child growing inside of her. And I sit in my normal spot at the other end. Although we are only a few feet apart, it still feels like there's miles between us.

"I'm sorry, Luke." I go to interrupt her but she holds her hand up to stop me. "Give me five minutes, let me try to make you understand why I've kept this from you. After that you can ask me whatever questions you want."

I give her a silent nod of the head and she continues, "I'm sorry. I know those words don't make up for the fact that I've kept this from you for five months, but you have to understand, in my head, I was doing this for you."

I promised her five minutes, but we are only about thirty seconds in and it's proving to be the most challenging thing yet today. "The night that you came here to tell me about the tour was the same night that I took just over a dozen pregnancy tests. Believe me when I say, I thought Charlie was crazy when she suggested that my symptoms reminded her of when she was pregnant with Tucker.

"Before you got here that night, I sat on this couch and felt excited. Excited to tell you that somehow our love overcame the impossible. I sat here knowing that even though having a child was the last thing on my mind, I instantly knew I loved this baby more than anything else in the world and the fact that you're the daddy, made it that much better. Not because you were on the verge of becoming some great, big, famous rockstar, but because you are you. Luke, you're one of the best people I know, and if this baby grows up to be even half as kind and loyal of a man as you are, he'll be an amazing person."

Her bottom lip starts to tremble in between words and I can tell that her tears are on the brink of bubbling over. "But when you got here that night, you were so excited about the tour and all the big things finally happening in your life. The moments you have dreamed about and worked hard for since you were a small child. I knew I couldn't tell you.

Her eyes drift down to where her fingers are drawing shapes on her belly, then return back to me. "Not because I didn't want to, believe me, I wanted you to lift me into the air, spin me around and then drop to your knees in front of me and declare your love for not only me, but also our baby. But I knew, just by the look of pure excitement in your eyes about the tour, that was not how it was going to play out. I knew you would stay out of obligation, that you would do the right thing even if that meant walking away from your dreams. And I didn't want that for you, I still don't want that for you.

"I was going to tell you, after that first tour, but then Walker announced at a friends dinner, that they had to hire a DJ for the wedding. He said you got booked to go on an even bigger tour that you couldn't turn down. I swear Luke, I was going to tell you before he got here… I was just waiting for the right time. Please don't hate me."

My brain is working overtime trying to process the information she just laid on me. I want to believe her, every bit of who I am wants to believe all the words that just came out of her mouth. But how can I trust her after this? She let me walk away that night after already knowing that she was carrying my child.

"He?"

"He what?" She looks up from her stomach and her red rimmed eyes find mine.

"You keep saying he? It's a boy then?"

Her one shoulder lifts slightly and she looks back down, "I don't know for sure. It didn't feel right to find out without you being there. So at my last ultrasound they checked everything out and made sure the baby was healthy but I asked the woman not to tell me the gender. I just keep having this dream of a little boy with sandy blonde hair and your perfect hazel eyes that change depending on what mood he's in. Just like his daddy." The last part comes out more like a soft whisper.

I stand up and walk across the living room to look out the floor to ceiling windows that overlook the lake. "Darlin' none of this was your decision to make. I'm the product of a mother who didn't want her child, do you think that I'd really walk away from you or him… her… whatever it is, if I'd known you were pregnant?"

She stands up and crosses the space between us, grabbing my arm to turn me so we're looking at each other. "No Luke, I knew without a doubt you wouldn't have left my side for one second if you knew. And I also know that if I'd let that happen, you'd someday resent me or the baby or maybe even both of us. And that's something I couldn't live with."

"And that guy tonight? That hulk-like meathead with his arm draped across your shoulder like he owned what was below it? The guy who DID get down on his knees to talk to your belly? Who's that?"

Her body starts to shake with laughter, as if any of this is funny. The woman I love more than anything in this world was being claimed by another man right in front of me tonight and there was nothing I could do about it. "Graham?" She starts to laugh again. "Meathead. He'll think that's great. And I can promise you, he wasn't *draped* over me because he's my older brother. He just moved home from the Army and his fiancé isn't here yet so he agreed to be my plus one."

"Your brother. Why in the hell did you continue to let me make a fool of myself tonight if you knew all along what I was thinking." I run my hands through my hair again, "God, Halee! Why are you so damn infuriating?"

" Me?! How about you rockstar, where's your date now that you're here talking to me. Considering that I have in fact already met your only sibling, I think we can rule out sister."

She's jealous, I can see it written all across her beautiful, moonlit face. "I reckon she's at the hotel. Probably even more confused about why she's there alone and not with me but at least it's a nice suite. I told her to order room service and put it on my card the hotel has on file."

"So I take it that you don't run by the same rules that you did before me? No sleepovers?"

"I don't really have any rules since you princess. Some mornings I wake up and I can't even remember the name of the woman or women that are laying next to me."

I realize by the flash of hurt that crosses her face what I just said was a low blow. But dammit she deserves it. She broke me. "I tried darlin', I tried to reach out to you so many times. You had so many chances to make this right and you didn't. Did you expect me to just sit around on my hands and wait for you to change your mind? To actually want me?"

Her back is to me now and the way that she is rubbing her stomach I can't tell if it's to console her or the baby. By the slight shake in her shoulders I can tell that she's crying, "Look Halee, I'm sorry. I didn't mean to hurt you, and trust me when I say that I want to be involved in this child's life from here on out. That means I will try my damnedest to fly home any chance I can for appointments. Just send me the dates and times. But as far as you and me, I don't know where we go from here. I don't know how I can trust you after this, and you don't deserve someone like me anyways. At least not the version of me that I've become. You broke me Halee, and I'm definitely not the same guy that walked out of this house five months ago."

"I'm. So. Sorry." She lets out in between sobs. "I-I never meant for this to play out this way. I thought I was doing what was best for you."

I walk up and wrap my arms around her from behind, placing my hands on her stomach, and feel the small miracle that's growing inside of her for the first time. My child. I press my lips to the top of her head, hopeful to indicate that everything is going to be ok. Even if I don't know if I believe it myself. "I know you're sorry. Friends. Remember you asked if we could be friends that night, I think maybe that's a good place for us to start. This baby is going to have the best set of parents in the entire world, even if we aren't together."

Halee's body trembles harder in my arms. I know that I'm breaking her right now, but I also know that I'm not physically or mentally capable of jumping back into 'us' again right away. Maybe not ever. When you give someone the ability to completely destroy you, and they do, I don't know if there's any coming back from that.

"I should probably take off. It's getting late and I have to be up early tomorrow to catch a plane back to Dallas. This is the last leg of this tour, so in about three weeks I'll be done for a couple of months."

"You're going back to that other woman?" She flips her body around in mine and this time we are so close I can feel the heat and sparks igniting between our two bodies.

I step back, trying to gain some control of the situation before I do something that I know I will regret in the morning. As much as I want to sleep with Halee, and boy do I want to, I also know that it would just blur the lines. "No Halee, I'm not going back to…"

"You don't even know her name Luke?"

"Yeah, I do, it's like Tiffany or Brittany or something like that. I've just been calling her Legs all night and she seemed excited to have a nickname."

She rolls her eyes, "Definitely living up to that rockstar title aren't ya." Halee doesn't wait for me to reply, "Don't go get a hotel room, it's already after midnight and I have an apartment over the garage that no one even uses. It's yours whenever you're in town."

I hesitate, the idea of being so close to her when I know that I can't have her. And like always she reads me like an open book. "Luke there is an entrance from the outside. You don't even have to come into the house. It's not being used and the furniture is all still up there from when Graham used to come to town. Just stay there."

I give her a nod, "Yea, that sounds good."

As I strip my clothes off and climb into bed my phone lights up on the nightstand. It's probably Annie freaking out because she just learned that I hopped on a plane and traveled across the country, thirty-five hours before our next show.

Princess: I'm sorry Luke. I know that it doesn't make it all go away. But I am.

Me: Go to sleep Halee. We can talk again soon.

I lean over to put the phone back just as it vibrates and lights up again.

Princess: Tell me a secret rockstar.

I know that she's trying, and I can appreciate her effort but I needed this five months ago. I start to type out my reply but delete it. She must once again sense that I'm struggling with what to say back because another text from her popped up.

Princess: Fine I'll go... I never stopped loving you. Not for one second that you were away. There has never been anyone else for me. Tell me that you don't still love me and I'll agree to be just friends with you. Tell me.

Me: I can't. But it doesn't matter Halee... sometimes loving someone isn't enough.

Me: Goodnight princess.

Chapter 27

Luke

February

Today we finished up the last leg of our tour and I'm boarding a plane, on my way back to Iron City. Other than discussing doctors appointments and the occasional 'How are you feeling' or 'Good luck at your show tonight' texts, Halee and I haven't talked much.

She hasn't asked me to tell her a secret since that night that we talked about everything and I haven't said it to her. My mind flashes back to that night, and how I tossed and turned in the bed of her apartment all night fighting with myself not to go down and crawl in behind her and tell her everything is going to be ok.

I love Halee, with every part of me. I love her so much it hurts. But she betrayed me, she made a decision that wasn't hers to make and although she may have done it with the idea that it was the right thing, it wasn't.

My sister is pissed. Demanding that we get a paternity test and insisting that this was all just a trap, that Halee made up the whole thing about not being able to have children naturally. But I know better. I also know that she wanted me there from the beginning, because after I got back on the road I called Walker. I wanted to know why the fuck he never called or texted me when he found out.

"Man, I'm so sorry. When I found out that Halee was pregnant, she told me the baby wasn't yours. She said that you knew she was pregnant but that you guys always used precautions and that the baby was from some random hook up. I just assumed that you were pissed off that she was sleeping around on the side so you left. None of us knew until the day after the wedding when Halee called us all over to her house and told everyone the truth. Other than Quinn and Charlie, who she made swear not to tell anyone, everyone thought that the baby was a result of

a one night stand." I can hear the honesty in Walkers voice as he talks. "I promise, if I would've known, you would've gotten a damn call from me telling you to get your ass back here."

I realize that I must be on speaker phone when Quinn starts to talk, "This is my fault Luke, I shouldn't have let her go through with this. But she was so persistent that it was what was best for you, and that she would tell you as soon as you got off tour, but then you started another one right away. That's why when Walker told me that you were coming to the wedding after all, I decided not to fill Halee in on the news. I didn't want to give her a chance to run from this. You needed to know."

I laugh, "I might know that I'm going to be a dad, but I have no fucking clue about what comes next." I stop and let out a long breath that I didn't realize I was holding in. "I don't know where her and I go from here."

"Do you still love her?" The female voice on the other end of the line asks.

"Quinn, stay out of this." Her husband tries to get her to back down, but knowing Quinn, she's just like Halee. When she has something on her mind, there's no stopping until she gets to the bottom of it.

"More than I've ever loved anyone else. But I don't know if I trust her enough to let her back in. She let me believe for five months that she didn't want me, god, she ignored all of my pleas for us to talk and try and make it work..."

Quinn stops me, "Don't give up on her Luke. Trust me when I tell you that it killed her going to those appointments without you. She wouldn't even let her parents or us girls go. Having a baby was never something she wanted, but I think it was because the doctors said that it would never happen. So her brain just tried to convince her body that it was ok this way. I know she's excited about becoming a mom, but my best friend hasn't shown much of any emotion when it comes to this pregnancy. She's scared Luke, she is scared of losing you, or even worse losing the baby. Even if you can't be with her, I need you to be there for her. Because her stubborn butt isn't going to admit when she needs someone, but I know that she needs you." Quinn stops for a second and I imagine she's looking at Walker when she continues, "Just like I needed the man sitting next to me."

"Ladies and gentlemen, as we start our descent, please make sure your seat backs and tray tables are in their full…" I didn't realize I was even tired until I closed my eyes after take off, but apparently I was, I never even heard the crew come around and ask if we wanted anything to drink.

✄✄✄

I walk into the small office that is filled to the brim with expectant mothers. Some of them are sitting next to a man, some another woman, and some of them are alone. After scanning the room, I find Halee sitting in the far corner reading one of the many parenting magazines scattered on the tables.

She looks up at me as I make my way towards her and her ocean like eyes light up like I'm the damn easter bunny. "Hey rockstar."

"Hey. Sorry I'm a little late. They thought my luggage was lost, so that took a bit to sort out." I lean down and kiss the top of her head before taking a seat in the empty chair next to her.

She gave me a sympathetic smile, "You're not late Luke, you are right on time." I feel like there is probably some sort of hidden meaning underneath that statement but before I can ask, a short middle aged woman opens the door and calls Halee's name.

"You ready to meet your kid?" She stands up, pulling me with her.

That seems like a loaded question that I don't really know the answer to. I always knew I wanted to be a dad, but I just thought it would be later in life. Later in my career. When I could afford to take some time off of touring, recording and small shows to help with a newborn. Not in the beginning of my career, when taking time off would do nothing but hurt me. If I'm not available, they will find some other up and coming to take my spot. It's a tough and grueling industry, but it's everything I have ever wanted.

We sit down in a small dark room that has a large screen on the wall. "I take it you're *dad* to our little Bean here?"

"Um... Bean?" I shoot Halee a questioning look.

Halee laughs, "When I had my first appointment, they told me that it was the size of a bean. So it stuck." She runs her hands over her stomach which looks even bigger than when I saw her three weeks ago. "My little Bean."

Her bottom lip finds its way to its happy place between her teeth. I can tell she's nervous, hell, if I stop and let myself think about it, I'm nervous. I try and give her a reassuring smile and look back at the doctor. "Yep, I'm the dad."

"Perfect. Halee had said that you had to be gone for work and that she wasn't sure when you were going to make it back in. You happen to be in luck, we are doing an ultrasound today to check on the baby's growth. Not only will you get to hear the heartbeat but you will get to also see this little miracle that you two have created." She pauses and looks back at Halee. "Does this mean we'll finally be finding out the gender today?"

Both sets of eyes turn to me again like I'm supposed to have all of the answers. "Oh, um… we actually haven't talked about if we wanted to find out. Luke? Do you want to know if it's a boy or a girl?"

I clear my throat, suddenly feeling like I need water, or better yet a shot of whiskey. "Ahh… I mean, I don't mind not knowing. Isn't that kinda part of the excitement?" When Halee doesn't say anything I continue, "But, if you want to find out, I'm ok with that too. Whatever you think is best."

She smiles, and turns back to the doctor. "I think we'll keep it a secret. Secrets are kind of our thing anyway." Her head turns back to me and she winks.

"Alright then, let's take a look at baby Bean and make sure he or she is developing all ten fingers and toes. Shall we?"

The doctor lifts up Halee's shirt and squirts this clear gel on her stomach. Next she pulls out a wand looking thing that is attached to the computer in front of her and places it on her stomach.

"Look." Halee says as she points to the large screen across the room. "That's our baby Luke."

I find it hard to draw my attention away from the woman that is sitting in front of me. Halee Thomas has always been beautiful in my eyes, but in this moment… she's the most stunning thing I have ever seen. The way that her entire body lights up, almost like she is glowing. Her eyes find mine when she realizes that I'm staring at her and not where she told me to look. "Luke."

"Huh?"

She grabs my knee with the hand closest to me, and with her other she points in the direction she wants my attention. "Look." She says, in almost a whisper.

When my eyes finally see what she's seeing, I melt. Even though I'm not one hundred percent sure on what exactly I'm looking at, I can tell that there's a head, hands and feet. It's a baby. It's my baby. And in that moment I know that I'm feeling exactly what's making Halee light up a room, excitement.

No matter the timing, and no matter what happens with me and this baby's mommy, I know that the most important person in my world is up on that screen. And I'm going to do my best at making sure it knows how loved he or she is.

I put my hand over Halee's and bring my eyes back to hers. "Yeah darlin', that's our baby."

Chapter 28

Halee

March

If I thought being away from Luke all those months was the hard part, I was greatly mistaking. The hard part is having him back, but him not really being here. It's been two weeks and our life consists of me going to work, Luke doing small shows or driving back to Chicago to do some recording in the studio, or us going to the baby appointments.

But other than when we go to the doctors and when we pass each other in the driveway, we don't really speak. Occasionally, he'll text and ask how I'm feeling, or if I need anything from the store when he goes, and vise versa. But that's it.

When he does come home, it isn't until the early hours, barely even beating the sun coming up.

This morning, I happen to glance out the kitchen window that overlooks the driveway just in time to see a busty blonde doing the walk of shame. My heart falls into my stomach and that dull ache that I've been feeling for the past few months intensifies.

I guess I don't know what I thought was going to happen when the truth came out about the pregnancy. The unrealistic part of me thought that maybe he would sweep me off my feet and we would live happily-ever-after with this perfect little miracle we created.

But even though my family and friends call me princess, my life isn't a fairy tale and Luke Taylor is not my knight in shining armor. In fact, him living in the apartment above the garage, and knowing what he's doing is actually more of my own personal hell.

The feelings of love that I knew were real, have started to fade and resentment has started to set in. I rest my hand on top of my growing belly as mixed emotions fill my head. How is it that I can be so excited to be a mommy to this little bean inside of me, but scared that one morning I'm going to wake up only to find out that this was all a dream. And the doctors were right, I can't really have children.

But now, I also have this weird feeling of sadness. Why now? And why with this man who clearly doesn't want me. He wants to be out on the road performing to the world and sleeping with random women every night.

I head out onto the back deck that overlooks the lake to finish my tea, and I look up into the sky. It's filled with oranges, purples, and blues as the sun makes its way into this new day.

"Mornin'."

His southern drawl is so much more prominent in the morning. I can't bring myself to turn and look at him, so I keep my gaze on the calming view in front of me. "Hey."

"You're up early." He walks up and sets his coffee cup next to mine on the railing.

"Yep."

"You feeling ok?" I can feel his intense stare burning into the side of my face.

"Yeah Luke, I'm fine." Letting out a deep breath, I take the last drink of my tea and turn around to head back inside and up to the safety of my own room. "Have a good day."

He grabs my elbow and stops me but I still don't dare turn to find out what color flecks dance in his hazel eyes today. "Halee…" His voice is almost a whisper as he lets go and turns back towards the lake.

In the reflection of the window in front of me I can see that he's wearing my favorite sweatpants that hang just right off of his hip bones. And his lack of a shirt is providing the ability to admire his perfectly toned back. For a moment, I begin to feel the heat building in between my legs, begging for a release that doesn't come from my own hand or my vibrator. But that feeling is shut down as soon as I remember that less than thirty minutes ago another woman was leaving him after a night of what I can only imagine was the best sex of her life.

I open the door that leads me back into the kitchen, suddenly feeling like I'm going to be sick. Barely making it to the bathroom down the hall, I throw up the tea and toast that I just ate.

I feel his presence behind me before he reaches down and pulls my hair back with one hand, rubbing my back with the other. "I thought you said that the morning sickness stopped after the first trimester."

When the pulling in my stomach lets up and it's safe to stand, I flush the toilet and make my way around Luke, to the sink to wash my hands and face.

Without answering him, I head out of the bathroom and make a break towards the stairs before his words stop me. "Really, Halee? I'm just trying to help. If you're having morning sickness, maybe there's something I can get you to help." His words are angry, like I'm the one that is doing something wrong.

"I'm fine Luke. Pretty sure that had nothing to do with the baby and everything to do with me seeing some blonde bimbo exiting the garage apartment this morning." His eyes widen but when he doesn't say anything I continue. "Do me a favor rockstar… go to their place, or fuck them in the backseat of your truck for all I care, but stop bringing them here. I get that you don't want me, and that's fine. I'm eight months pregnant and I look like a beached whale most days, why wouldn't you choose the women who still have bangin' bodies with flat stomachs. But it isn't fair to me to have to be reminded constantly by you parading women around. Not to mention, this is my house after all."

His hands work their way through his messy hair that needs cut, and land on his neck. "Halee..." He lets out a long sigh and his eyes find mine, "You're beautiful. You're the most gorgeous woman I've ever laid eyes on, don't think for one second that you aren't. That belly, and the way that your tiny hands always seem to find their way to it, even when you don't realize what you're doing. It's perfect. You are perfect, princess."

The tears that I've been trying so hard to hold back since I looked out the kitchen window this morning finally come. "You don't get to say things like that to me Luke, and then do the things you keep doing. It's fine that you don't want me, and I know you're only here for the baby. But maybe you should leave. This..." I point between the two of us, "isn't healthy. Not for me, not for you and definitely not for our child."

"What do you mean leave? Halee, I'm not walking away from my own kid, did you forget that I know exactly what that feels like and I will be damned if you think for one second that I'll do the same. I want *Bean* more than I've wanted anything in this world. Even more than music."

The fact that he called him Bean, makes my heart soften a little. "Look, I'm not saying you should walk away forever. But I am saying that you should go back to Chicago, figure out what you want, because this baby is going to be here in less than two months. At this point, we don't have anymore ultrasounds, it's basically all just check ups to make sure I'm measuring normal. My mom can go with me if it makes you feel better that I'm not alone." I can't figure out what he's looking at on the wall behind me, or if he has heard anything that I just said to him. "Just go, Luke. You're hurting me more by being here then if you were just gone."

"So that's it? Just walk away. That's what you want me to do."

No.

My heart tells me to scream at him and tell him that what I want is him. I want us. Like we were before tour dates and baby appointments became our new reality. I want to lay in bed all day making love, only getting up when one of us has to pee or when we need food. But my brain speaks louder than my heart when it reminds me that he doesn't want me like that anymore. That I ruined any chance we had at a happily-ever-after, the moment I let him walk out of here without telling him that he was going to be a father. My brain reminds me that he doesn't want someone like me.

So as much as it breaks me to say the next words, I know I have to. "Just leave, Luke. I want you to leave."

"Halee-" His voice broken, and the dam holding back his tears breaks. "I'm sorry, princess."

"Me too, rockstar, me too." And I turn, leaving him and what was left of my heart in the living room. Once I'm in my bedroom, I sit on the edge of the bed and wait. Part of me hopes he'll run after me, burst through my bedroom door and tell me that he isn't leaving. Tell me that he's going to stay today, and every day after this because he can't imagine spending another minute without me. But the rational part of me, the part that just heard the front door close, knows this is what's best. Even if it doesn't feel that way right now.

I don't know where we go from here, and I don't know what will happen in six weeks when this baby comes and I have to deal with him being around. And worse, possibly bringing other women around me and Bean. But what I do know is I need my girls…

The Girls: SOS

I lay my phone on the bed next to me, lay back and let my tears fall. My heart broke all those months ago when I told him to leave, but back then I thought we still had a chance at a future. Now, it's shattered into a million pieces because I know that we're over. That this sweet, perfect and innocent child growing inside of me is going to enter this world into an already broken family. With an already broken mommy.

"I'm sorry, Bean." My fingers draw out the words *I love you* on the top of my belly. "I've failed you this time, but I promise, I won't let it happen again."

My phone vibrates on my side.

Charlie: Dropping Tuck off with Walker. Quinn and I will be there in twenty minutes.

I set my phone down just as it vibrates again.

Luke: I'm sorry, Halee. I never meant for you to see another woman leaving, and I can't even begin to imagine how that made you feel. I would be seeing red if I had to watch another man walk out of your house before sunrise. Knowing that he got to hold you all night, and listen to the sweet whispers you let out while you sleep. I'm broken Halee... no longer the man that you knew before. I don't know if I can ever be that person again. I'm leaving, but

before I do, you have to know something. I love you. I'll always love you, until the day I die. And I'll love that little baby we magically, against all odds, created that is growing inside of you.

Luke: You deserve so much more than me.

Luke: I'm only a phone call or text away Halee... If you need me, just say the words and I'm here. Goodbye for now princess.

Before I could reply and beg him to stay, I turn my phone off and throw it into the bedside drawer. I don't have to be a functioning adult until Tuesday at work. That gives me two more days to avoid the reality that I just officially became a single mom.

Chapter 29

Halee

"So wait, he had another woman over here? And you watched her do the walk of shame?" Charlie is sitting on the bar stool at the corner of my kitchen island.

When they arrived, Luke was already long gone and as for me, I was still laying in bed crying, trying to figure out how I got myself into this mess. Maybe if I would have just told him up front about the baby, maybe then we wouldn't be where we are right now. But I still stand by the fact that he would have stayed out of obligation, not because he wanted to. Then where would that land us? Five, maybe ten years down the road he resents me and the baby for keeping him from his dreams?

I try not to think too hard about the night that I met the mesmerizing Luke Taylor, because when I do, part of me regrets even staying with him. I should've stuck to my guyatus and walked back out into that bar, let a few more guys buy me drinks in hopes that their pick up lines would get them laid. And then got my drunk ass back into Quinn's jeep and came back home.

If I'd never met him, I would've never fallen for him and the sweet way his southern charm rolls out of his mouth.

But then I wouldn't have been given the biggest blessing in the world. Almost as if Bean knew I was thinking about him, I feel a swift kick to the ribs.

"Earth to Halee?"

"Sorry, what did you say?"

Quinn is standing over the stove cooking up the burger for tacos while I prepare all of the extra fixings. "We were talking about the walk of shame you had to witness this morning… I'm sorry Hales. I don't know why he would think it's ok to bring someone else back to your home."

I shrug my shoulders and continue on cutting up the lettuce. "I don't know guys. But maybe him leaving is for the best. You know? Maybe we just aren't meant to be together."

When I look up, I see the sadness stretched across my friends' faces. And instead of them reassuring me that everything is going to be ok, I spend the next twenty minutes explaining how it's all going to work out. The nursery furniture will be here next week, and since the room is already in grey tones I have decided to just add pops of turquoise so it will go along with whatever gender the baby ends up being.

"You guys are going to have to figure this out eventually. Whether you are together or not together, at the end of the day you are still going to be co-parenting." Quinn's telling me everything that my mom and dad have been saying for weeks. And I know they're all right, I know that he and I are going to have to sit down and be adults at some point. But today, the day that I realized the man I fell in love with is not the man I thought he was, didn't seem like a great time to open up that can of worms.

"Okay!" I clap my hands in front of me. "New rule, no more talking about how much *Halee* has screwed up her life. We're going to finish making this kick ass taco bar, you bitches are going to drink margaritas and we're going to watch chick flicks until it's time for you to go back home to your families. I'm going to be ok." I place my hand on its new favorite place and my thoughts go to what Luke said earlier about how I'm most beautiful when my hand is on my belly. "*We* are going to be ok."

Both of the girls give me a smile that says they're trying to be supportive but they know the hard times are still ahead of me. And I know they are right. But for today, I want to forget my problems, and I want to have a girls day with my best friends.

And that's exactly what we do.

Chapter 30

Luke

On my way back to Chicago my phone screen lights up with Walkers name on it. I figured that as soon as I left, Halee called Quinn, who probably told Walker and now I was about to get my ass chewed for being such a ginormous fuck up.

I click the answer button on the screen on my dash, "Hey, Walker."

"What the fuck did you do?" His voice sounds stern coming through the speakers, but not as pissed off as I was expecting.

"Well, should I start at the beginning or just last night when I made a huge mistake and got super sloppy drunk. I don't remember much after my set, but I woke up next to a naked blonde. And for the record, it wasn't the naked blonde that's carrying my baby. Oh! And to make things worse, I immediately told the blonde that she needed to leave, hoping Halee was still sleeping. But as luck would have it, she watched the woman leave through the kitchen window."

The line stays silent so I glance down to make sure that we didn't get disconnected.

"Duuuude… Your telling me you brought some groupie back to Halee's house and banged her? What in the hell is wrong with you Luke?"

I laugh, "Well that's the thing, I'm pretty sure we didn't sleep together because as she was throwing things at me while getting dressed she said something like 'worst night of her life' and that I couldn't even get it up and I apparently kept calling her Halee."

I don't give him a chance to talk before I continue, "And as far as what is wrong with me…

that's quite a long list. Starting with I'm pretty sure I just lost any chance of getting Halee back. Ever."

Now it's Walker's turn to laugh, "Do you even want her back? Halee was over the other day and she made it seem like you haven't even been showing her the slightest bit of interest. Besides going to the doctors appointments, she told us that you guys don't even really talk."

I think about his words and I replay the past few weeks of my life in my head. I know that we've been keeping a lot of distance between the two of us, but have I been shutting her out so much that I missed any sign that she wanted to work on things?

Ever since the night that I told her I didn't know if love was enough, she never brought the idea of us being together back up. "She's everything man." Now stuck in a traffic jam just outside the city, I roll my windows down and take in the unaverage heat that surprised everyone for mid March. "I wake up thinking about her, fall asleep wondering if she's thinking about me too, and dream of her and what our life could be while I sleep."

"Where are you?"

"About thirty minutes outside of Chicago."

"Why?" His question confuses me, considering he knows where I live.

"Ah… because I live here."

"I know you live there dip shit, but what I don't know is why you walked away from the woman that you love."

"Because. She said me being there was just hurting her more and after everything that she has been through, I can't stand to hurt her anymore than I already have."

"You're an idiot. But you know what, do whatever you want. Just take some advice from me. When a woman tells you to leave, most of the time she really means 'stay and fight for us'. Life is too short for the two of you to being playing these bullshit, cat and mouse games with each other. You want her, she wants you, and by some crazy miracle, your super sperm got her pregnant when everyone said it couldn't happen. If that isn't a sign then I don't know what is."

"Since when are you all spiritual about signs and shit?"

He laughs, "Right around the time my life brought me to a small town called Iron City to fill a position of a fallen firefighter whose fiancé is now my extremely sexy wife. Life has a way of showing you where you are supposed to be. But it's up to you whether or not you follow the signs."

"Yeah, well we aren't you and Quinn. And we all don't always get our happily-ever-after."

"Just think about it Luke. The only person standing in the way of your dream girl and a family is you. But I got to go, Tucker's movie just got over so we are going to head outside and play."

"Ok, but Walker."

"Yeah."

"Thanks for calling."

"I always have your back, even when I think you are being a complete fuck up." And with that, he hangs up the phone, leaving me to my thoughts for the rest of the drive home.

Chapter 31

Luke

"What are you doing here?" My sister Annie looks up from her laptop and glares.

"Jesus, why is it that people seem to be forgetting I fucking live here. I'm going to go jump in the shower, we can talk later." I set my guitar case down by the front door and carry the rest of my stuff to my room.

"Whatever you say baby brother, but that looks like you packed for a more permanent stay rather than a quick trip like you have been doing. Did something happen with Halee? Is the baby ok?"

"Baby's fine Annie. Just let me take a shower and we can talk."

I'm pretty sure I could still hear her mumbled words as I shut the door to my room. She's right, when I left today I wasn't sure if I would ever be allowed to stay at Halee's again so I packed everything I had there. But sitting in my bedroom now, in the house that has been my home for over three years, it doesn't feel like I belong here anymore.

My whole world is back in Michigan and I just drove away like an idiot, without even putting up a fight.

Walker was right, I love Halee. There's never been a moment of doubt in my mind whether or not I cared deeply for that woman. But how do we get back to the way we used to be? How do I just jump back into what we had and trust that from this point forward she's going to talk to me before making life altering decisions?

She was right, I would've stayed if I'd known then what I know now. But I wouldn't have given up on my dream. What makes her think that her and this baby couldn't be part of the dream with me. There are plenty of musicians out there that live that dream every day. They rock out to hundreds of thousands of people, singing their music and making people feel everything with the words that they write, and then they go home to their family.

I know she thinks she would eventually not be enough, but what she doesn't understand is that she has everything I've ever wanted. Halee Thomas is the dream. So the question remains, what am I doing here, in my two bedroom house that I now share with my sister when deep down I know my heart is in Iron City?

What it comes down to is, I changed the night when I left her and went out on tour, becoming a man that I myself don't even recognize. She deserves better than someone like me. That man is exactly who she was worried I would be once I was out on the road. The drinking, the women and the nights that Annie had to peel me off of the floor to make sure I made it to my tour bus safely.

The moment I found out the truth, that Halee was pregnant, was the day I decided to be better. I slowed down on the drinking and I haven't had sex with another woman since. Not to say that my friend that hangs out between my legs hasn't tried to encourage me when women throw themselves at us. But instead of giving in, I continue to find relief with my hand in the shower. Which is exactly what I am doing right now.

As the warm water hits my chest I slowly stroke my hand up and down my throbbing shaft all while my mind thinks about the ocean blue eyes that consume my dreams. The way her plump bottom lip always finds its way to its happy place between her teeth and how it pulls when she's just at the peak of her orgasm. I think about her tits and how they used to bounce up and down in my face when she was riding my cock, and how much fuller they'd feel now between my hands while I pulled and nibbled on her nipples. I find my release just as I'm picturing the way her hand always makes its way to her delicate nub when I'm teasing her and not giving her the release she desires. "Fuck…"

But after my own climax I open my eyes to the disappointing reality that I'm alone, in a shower, and the star of my fantasy is in a whole other state.

✂✂✂

"So let me get this straight… You wanted her, but she pretended not to want you so that you would go out into the world and live your dream. Then you find out she lied to you about the pregnancy and tell her that you just want to be friends. Then she tells you that she loves you and wants to be more than friends and you tell her you don't think that is possible anymore. Then your dumbass gets drunk and brings another woman home, she sees her and kicks you out. Does that pretty much sum up the past eight months of your life?"

"Yep." I take a swig of my beer to wash down the last bite of my pizza. "That seems pretty accurate."

Annie lets out a belly laugh that shakes her entire body. "You two really know how to make shit difficult don't ya. Like a dog chasing its tail. You love her, and she loves you. You guys are going to have a baby soon but you're so stuck in your own heads that you can't even seem to get out of the way of love."

"Whoa, whoa, whoa." I hold my hand up to stop her wisdom on love advice. "What exactly happened to you? Less than two months ago she was nothing but a 'gold digging groupie' that you kept saying you warned me not to get involved with. What gives Annie?"

She looks down at her empty plate and then back at me with sad eyes. "I don't know Luke, lots of things. I've been thinking, and I talked to pops and we think that this is a good thing. After seeing the way that you reacted when you left out on tour, with the drinking and random hook ups. If you continued down that road, I would hate to think about how you'd end up. After talking to Halee-"

"Wait! When the fuck did you talk to her Annie?" I'm up off the stool I was just sitting on and now pacing throughout the kitchen.

"Don't get mad little brother, I was just doing my job as your manager and more importantly your big sister. I needed to know that this woman you let so easily into your heart was worth it." I open my mouth to tell her it's none of her fucking concern whether or not Halee is worth it. But before I can get the words out she holds her hand up to me. "Stop! Whatever you are thinking, just stop. And listen. I called her shortly after you told me that she was pregnant, and to be honest with you, I discovered a whole new respect for her and what she did. Did she lie to you? Yes. But Luke, I think she was truly just doing what she thought was best for you. It takes a strong woman to let the man that she loves, walk out of her life at the exact moment she needed you most. She endured months of morning sickness, going to doctors appointments and dealing with the local gossip, alone."

"Annie, I never asked her to deal with all of that shit alone. I would've been there, googling remedies to help with morning sickness, holding her hand at every damn doctors appointment and telling everyone who had something negative to say to fuck off. I would've been there sis, for all of it."

She comes over and brings my now shaking body into a hug just like she used to do when I was younger and would cry about mom leaving. The only difference is that now I tower over her tiny frame, and back then she was still a little bigger than me. "I know you would have, and so does she. But if you would've been there, you wouldn't have been doing two major tours. You wouldn't have three labels after you for possible recording deals, you would still be playing in night clubs and hole in the wall bars, Luke. And I know you were always ok with that, but you don't see yourself through our eyes. You're so much greater than that. You were born to be on the big stages with thousands of fans screaming your name and singing your music. Thanks to Halee and her willingness to sacrifice a few months without you, all of those things are going to happen for you. As far as I'm concerned, that woman is a saint. Not only does she love you, but she let you walk away, hoping you would eventually come back to her."

"I'm not so sure she loves me anymore, Annie. You should've seen her face this morning when she told me that I was doing nothing but hurting her by being there. She thinks I slept with the girl from last night."

Annie sits back down at the island and I follow her lead, taking my seat again. She gives me her know it all smirk that she has basically mastered over the years of giving me advice. "Well, did you happen to fill her in on the fact that you not only did not sleep with that woman but you have also managed to keep your snake in your pants since the moment you found out the truth?"

"No. I didn't think she would believe me. I mean, even I wouldn't believe me if I was her. The night of Walker's wedding when I went back to Halee's to talk, I told her that I had basically slept my way through the tour. Shit Annie, I even told her about the weird ass threesome I woke up to but couldn't seem to remember."

"You're disgusting, Luke. I mean, seriously, what the hell's wrong with you?"

My elbows rest on the counter and my head falls into the palms of my hands. "I reckon I was just trying to hurt her, like she hurt me. Definitely wasn't my finest hour."

"You don't say. So now what? What happens next?"

"Now I try and figure out how I get my girl back." Hopefully she hasn't given up on me yet. I make a promise to myself as I make my way back to my room, if I can get her back, I'll never walk away from her or our baby ever again.

I pick up my phone, hoping I still know the way to her heart.

Me: Tell me a secret princess…

Chapter 32

Halee

It's Tuesday morning and I actually do have to be a functioning adult today. I have to drag my butt into the shower, get dressed in real adult clothes, and do something with my hair other than throwing it up into a messy bun on top of my head.

After an hour, I finally feel like I'm presentable enough to leave the house and join the rest of the human population whose world didn't shatter over the weekend. As I walk out of my room to head downstairs, I remember that my phone's still in the drawer of my bedside table where I put it Saturday morning.

It was hard. Really hard not to turn it on, but I knew that if I did I would just be stalking Luke's social media accounts or looking at old pictures or even worse calling him. I just needed a couple of days of peace and to help myself realize that it's ok that I'm not enough for him. He needs someone who wants to be on the road all the time and is ok with picking her life up to follow him all over the country, and that person is not me. My life is here, in Iron City.

Of course I would have been willing to go on trips occasionally, I love watching Luke perform and to see him work a crowd the magical way he does. But none of that matters now, he's better off without someone like me tying him down.

Me and little Bean are going to be just fine on our own. I know that Luke will try and be here as much as he can while he isn't on the road. And I wouldn't dream of trying to keep him away. I know he's going to be the best dad ever. But it's important to me that our baby grows up as normal as possible, even if his daddy is some big rockstar.

When my phone screen comes to life, it instantly starts vibrating with incoming texts…

Q: Hey, your phone is going straight to voicemail when I call. I'm assuming it's just turned off and you are not dead inside that

giant house of yours. See you Tuesday at work. If you don't show up, I'm sending out a search party... aka JR and Walker. Love you Hales.

Charlie: Are you alive? I'm here if you need me girl.

Charlie: Who run the world? Girls! (In my best Beyonce voice). You got this, you don't need a man. *wink face emoji* Hearts babe

JR: Do I need to find a certain country music star and kick his ass? Rumor has it that you locked yourself in your house. Don't make me swim across the lake. But for real, you know where to find me if you need me.

My stomach drops when I get to the next text notification.

Rockstar: Tell me a secret princess...

Rockstar: I've tried calling. Several times. Then I resorted to calling Quinn to make sure everything was ok because you were starting to worry me. She basically ripped my dick off through the phone and made me eat it. I'm sorry Halee. I want to talk to you. Please call me.

Rockstar: Ok I will tell you a secret. You are everything I have ever wanted, and so is the miracle we created that's growing inside of you. I want you Halee Sue Thomas, and I wish that I wasn't doing this through a text but I know you don't want to see me right now so I'm not sure what other choice I have. I don't want to be your friend, I want to be your everything. Please give me a chance to explain. Call me princess. Please.

My heart drops into my stomach as I read his words. But then my mind shoots back to a few weeks ago when I all but threw myself at him and he basically told me that our love wasn't enough.

If he didn't believe in what we had and think it was enough back then, what has changed now? I have spent my whole life putting everything into my relationships with men, just to get shit on in the end. I don't know if I can do it this time.

I know that we are going to have some sort of relationship for the sake of Bean but maybe a close friendship and co-parenting is all we were meant to have. And regardless of how badly it hurts, I have to pull my crap together and get on with my day-to-day life. Not only for me but for the baby. I love Luke. I love him so much it hurts, but at the end of the day I have to love myself more. I have to understand that just me and the simple life that comes with me probably will never be enough for him. He's a damn rockstar. And even though he might not be huge now, I have zero doubt that his time is coming. I knew the consequences of my actions the day I agreed to see where this could go. Leave it to me, Halee Thomas, to fall in love with someone that is just about as emotionally unavailable as they get.

✂✂✂

The smell of perm assaults my nose as I walk into Studio 365. It's funny how much things change when you are pregnant, and the smell of perms is definitely one of them. They didn't use to affect me at all, in fact, I'd almost even say the smell of them relaxed me, made me feel unusually comfortable. But now, it's taking everything in me not to run into the bathroom and lose the avocado toast that I ate this morning.

"Oh good, you're here. Charlie call off the dogs, we don't have to send the search and rescue team out for Halee." Quinn shouts to the other room while she busys herself washing out her color bowl.

"Haha, very funny." I start to unload my work bag and put my lunch into the fridge when she stops me.

"Really though, all jokes aside, how are you doing?" The look of concern stretched across her face is genuine. Her eyes are extra green today and the way she's looking at me almost feels like she can read through all of my bullshit that I was just about to spit at her. So I decide to skip that part and just give her the truth that she would've eventually gotten out of me anyways.

"I'm ok. I mean…" I pause to think about how I want to word this without sounding completely pathetic. "I'm about as good as I think I'm going to be. I'm eight months pregnant, I feel like a whale, I can barely bend over to put my shoes on and girl I'm scared to see how my lady parts look because I haven't been able to properly shave in weeks."

She lets out a contagious laugh and we both are almost crying laughing at the image I just drew for her. "Well princess, I love you. But that's where I draw the line. I am NOT shaving your beaver."

I slap her on the arm, "Gross Q, beaver! What's wrong with you? And don't worry, it's not like anyone is going to be seeing me beside the doctor anytime soon. I'm not really that worried about it."

Her smile falls and I can tell she's battling with what to say next. She takes a deep breath and exhales it out. "You know he called me right?"

I nod my head and look away as my eyes start to blur over. She wraps her arms around me, "If it's any consolation, I really let him have it. And Walker called him too. I think he realizes now how badly he screwed up Hales. Have you talked to him?" I shake my head this time continuing to avoid her sympathetic eyes. "Well maybe you should, he seems pretty tore up about it all."

I can't believe what I am hearing come out my best friends mouth. Is she really going to bat for the guy who not only rejected me a few months ago, but also stays out all night with other women and then took it to the extreme of bringing one of the women home… to my home. Anger takes over my body and I can feel my hands start to tremble. "I know you are not taking his side with this. What, are you suddenly *Team Luke*?"

She steps back from me and throws her hands up like she is surrendering, "Whoa, whoa, whoa, I am and will always be Team Halee. But I also want you to be happy, and I really think that the two of you can be happy. If you just get out of your own way and let each other back in." She steps back towards me and puts both hands on my shoulders, "Those few months before you found out that you were pregnant and before Luke left, you were the happiest I've ever seen you. You two were made for each other, you just have to get back to the place you used to be."

"I don't even know if that is possible Q-" a sharp pain stabs me in my abdomen and I fall forward catching myself on the counter in front of me. "-oh God."

"Halee! Halee what's wrong?" The pain takes over the lower half of my body, I reach for the closest chair in an attempt to sit. "Hales, talk to me. What's going on?"

"Somethings wrong Quinn. Something's really wrong." My hands are gripping my stomach, and all I can think about are the worst case scenarios that have been invading my thoughts since I found out I was pregnant. "I think I need to go to the hospital… oh god, Quinn, what if something's wrong? What if the baby-"

She puts her hand up and stops me from even finishing that sentence. "Halee, the baby's fine, you are going to be fine. Let's get you to the hospital so they can figure out what's going on. Stay here for a second, I'm going to go tell Charlie what's going on and see if she can cancel the rest of both our days. Be back in thirty seconds."

"Yea, I don't see me going anywhere too fast." As she rushes out of the back room I grab my phone out of my work bag.

Me: I need you Luke.

Chapter 33

Luke

Princess: I need you Luke.

I set my guitar down and tell the guys I need a minute. We've been in this damn stuffy recording studio for about three hours and nothing seems to be coming out right.

"What the hell are you doing Luke?" Annie sticks her head out the door as I make my way down the hallway to head outside.

"I need five, I have to make a phone call." I shout over my shoulder without stopping.

"Well when you get back, hopefully your head will be removed from your ass because whatever you're doing in there isn't working."

I throw one hand up in the air and bring the one holding my phone up to my ear. "Yep!"

The phone goes straight to voicemail and for a second I consider leaving a message asking what the hell her text was about. But a feeling inside me is saying that something's wrong. I click the end button and find Quinn's name in my contacts. It rings three times that feel like an eternity before she picks up. "Hi, Luke." Shit, it sounds like she's crying.

"What's wrong Quinn, are they ok?" I find myself reaching into my pocket hoping my truck keys are in there. Fuck. I'm pretty sure I threw them on the table next to my guitar case when I got here. I start to jog inside as I hear her gentle sobs on the other end of the line. "Damn it, say something. Please tell me they're ok."

"Y-yea, Halee is okay." She chokes out in between her staggered breaths. I hear a man's voice in the background and assume it must be

Walker, he says something like 'give me the phone so I can tell him what's going on.'

I swing the door open to the recording studio and everyone's heads turn in my direction. When I snag my keys off the table and start running back out the door I hear Annie yell, "Where do you think you're going? We still have another two hours that have already been paid for."

"I gotta go Annie, something is wrong with Halee and the baby."

Just when I make it out the door a man's voice that I don't recognize gets on the other end of the line. "Hey Luke, this is Graham, we met briefly at Quinn and Walkers wedding. I think you might've thought I was Halee's date and not her brother..."

"Yeah. What the hell's going on. Are they ok?"

My sister opens my driver side door, directing me with her hands to move over. "You shouldn't be driving. I'll drive you there."

I mouth the words 'thank you' while I listen to Graham explain that when Halee got to work today, she started to experience severe abdominal pain and by the time she reached the hospital they noticed that she was also having some light bleeding. "Halee's going to be fine, but they're back doing some tests to make sure that the baby is ok and that they don't need to do an emergency c-section."

"Isn't it too early to deliver? She is just barely thirty-six weeks." I run my fingers through my hair as I stare out the front window, I can tell that Annie keeps looking in my direction waiting for answers just like I am.

"Well... " He pauses and take a deep breath. "Yes and no. The survival rate is quite high at thirty-six weeks but obviously the longer the little Bean stays in there, the better."

"I'm on my way. I should be there within two hours. If anything changes please call me. Is she alone?" Guilt hits me like a mack truck, I should've been there with her. I should be holding her hand and telling her everything is going to be ok. I should've never left the other day when she told me she needed space. Damn it, I should've fought for her, for us. A single tear rolls down my face and I feel my sister's hand reach over and touch my arm.

"She isn't alone, my mom is back there with her. Just get your ass here. And Luke."

"Yeah."

"If you ever hurt my sister again, I promise you, they won't even find your body." Knowing what he used to do while he was enlisted in the Army, I have no doubt that he could kill me off and no one would even begin to know where to look for me.

"Got it. See you soon." The call ends before I even have a chance to say anything else.

I let out a long breath that I am pretty sure has been trapped inside of me since I read Halee's text message. "Wanna talk about it?" My sisters voice pulls me out of the nightmare that is taking place inside my head.

"I should've never left, Annie. What the fuck was I thinking?" Running the palms of my hands down my face and leaning my head back into the seat, I try to gain control of my breathing.

"Well baby brother, I guess you were probably thinking that the woman you love just told you that you being around was causing her more pain than good." I look over at her and she briefly takes her eyes off the road and gives me a sympathetic smile. "But now you need to get your shit together. You're going to be a dad, and from the sound of that conversation, you might be holding your son or daughter today. It's time to make some decisions… do you love Halee?"

I don't even need time to think about my answer to that question. "More than anything."

"So tell her that. Make this work. Not only for the baby or for Halee, but for you. Luke, you deserve all the happiness in the world and I think that this woman was sent to you for a reason." I go to give her shit about how much has changed since the first time she met Halee, just less than a year ago. "Don't talk, just listen. I've never been one to believe in soulmates, especially after all the crap that happened with pops and mom. But this woman showed up at one of your shows, drew your attention out of all the other women practically throwing themselves at you that night, then she ended up being best friends to Walker's fiancé. You two hit it off, and against all the odds in the world end up making this little miracle baby, even though she was told it could never happen. She completes you, Luke. I never saw you smile in your entire life like you did when the two of you were together. You guys were supposed to meet, you were meant to start a family, and if that doesn't scream soulmate, then I don't know what does."

I'm smiling by the time she is done with her typical big sister lecture. "Can I talk now?"

"Only if you don't say anything stupid." She says with a lazy smile.

"I'm going to get my girl back, Annie. I have to make things right between us."

Chapter 34

Halee

"Bedrest?!? No way... there's no way that I can lay in bed for the next four weeks. I'll go crazy." I look between the doctor and my mom, waiting for them to tell me that this is all a big joke. "You aren't kidding, are you?"

"I'm afraid not." Doctor Johnson says, "After what happened today, we can't take any chances. Although the bleeding has stopped and you're no longer experiencing abdominal pains, that doesn't mean you're in the clear. You need to relax, keep your stress levels down, and most importantly, stay in bed. As long as you can promise me that you will do this, I'm willing to release you."

My mom places her hand on my hand, "This isn't up for negotiation, Halee. You want that sweet little baby to stay in there until it's time for him or her to come out, right?"

I nod my head, knowing this is what's best for my baby. But it still doesn't make the idea of being confined to my bed for the next thirty or so days any easier. "Then it's settled, I will move in with you to help out until the baby is born."

"You don't have to do that. I can move in with her." I would recognize his deep raspy voice anywhere. When I turn to look at the doorway that is currently filled with the most beautiful man I've ever seen, I instantly notice his hazel eyes have a redness around the rim. He's been crying.

Doctor Johnson turns to look at Luke and she asks, "And you are?"

Luke holds his hand out to her, "Luke Taylor, the father." He walks across the room and places a light kiss on my temple and whispers 'hey princess' in my ear so only I can hear. The feeling of his warm breath on my skin sends chills throughout my entire body causing me to squeeze my thighs together. "Mrs. Thomas, I'm able to take care of Halee. You don't have to move in. I've got her."

He winks at me and I can feel the heat radiating off of every surface of my body. Doctor

Johnson clears her throat, "Well then, it's settled. I will begin your discharge papers." She stands up and smooths the wrinkles out of her white coat. "Oh and one more thing, you also need to avoid…" she clears her throat as if she is uncomfortable with whatever she's about to say next. "You need to avoid any penetration. No sex."

My mom follows the doctor out of the room after saying that she will give us a minute alone and go tell our family in the waiting area what's going on.

When the door shuts, my eyes make their way back up Luke's body. Starting with his worn boots, ripped dark denim jeans, his simple black henley that hugs his muscles perfectly and I land on his mesmerizing, brownish, green eyes. "Thanks for coming."

He brushes the stray hairs that have fallen from my messy bun out of my face. "I should've never left you in the first place. I'm sorry, Halee. I know I've messed up a lot lately, but I want to make it up to you. Please let me make this better."

I sit forward on the bed, adjusting the back of the hospital gown so that my ass isn't hanging out. "We both have made a lot of mistakes, Luke. How about we try and start over. Friends?"

I don't want to be his friend. The voices inside my head are yelling at me, telling me to take it back. But I also know that if I'm not careful, I could end up exactly where I started. "Friends?!" Luke looks at me with disbelief. "Halee, I don't just want to be your friend. In fact, I can't *just* be your friend ever again."

"I know Luke, but hear me out. Let's take this slow, get to know each other all over again, build a solid foundation and see where that leads us. We have, give or take, thirty days to get our crap together before our lives change drastically. Plus, you heard the good doctor, no penetration. So us trying this just friends thing is a good way to make sure things don't go too far. Deal?"

He leans down and brings his forehead so it's touching mine. "Whatever you say darlin', but in case you forgot, I don't need to penetrate in order to have you shaking and screaming out my name." And he leans down and places the sexiest kiss just below my ear on my neck. "Get dressed, princess. Let's go home."

When he leaves me alone in the room, I take a couple minutes to get my breathing under control. He's going to play dirty, and that's fine.

Two can play that game.

Chapter 35

Halee

"Why don't you go upstairs and change into something comfortable and I'll make us some dinner."

It's been four hours since he walked into that hospital room and somehow weaved himself right back into my life and more so, my home.

I mean, I see the irony of the situation. He's kind of a permanent fixture in my life for at least the next eighteen years. And if I'm being practical here, probably even longer than that. Someday I'm sure that Bean will get married, and they'll have children of their own and I'll be stuck constantly running into the only man who has ever truly owned my heart.

His calloused hand brushes across my arm, "Darlin'. Did you hear me?" When our eyes meet but I don't give him an answer, he continues. "Go on up and put on something comfortable, maybe even take a bath. I'll cook dinner, and bring it up when it's done."

"Yeah, that sounds good. But you don't have to bring it up to me, I can come back down here." I start to walk towards the stairs but his hand finds my arm and stops me.

"Halee, please don't fight me on this. I'm here to help, and you heard what the doctor said. You need to stay in bed as much as possible and try to avoid the stairs." He reaches up and pushes a strand of hair behind my ear that must have fallen forward. "We need to keep that little rascal inside of you for a few more weeks so that he or she is ready for this crazy world."

"I know Luke, but what am I supposed to do in that damn bed for four more weeks. I'm going to go stir crazy, and not to mention the salon…"

Before I can finish, his lips find mine, the feeling of want and desire spreads through me like wildfire. This is the connection that I've been missing all these months. This is what makes me feel alive after all this time of feeling alone, empty and dead. This is everything I want… but the realization of what we are doing snaps me out of whatever realm that we were just existing in and brings me back to the real world. "We can't do this, Luke." I step away but he follows. "Luke…" My words come out breathy and unconvincing.

"Princess, if you can look me in the eyes right now and tell me you didn't just feel that. That it didn't just feel like your entire body was lit on fire when our lips touched, then I promise I will back away now and we'll only be friends from here on out." My eyes move from his almost grey iris's, down to his lips and back up again. I feel my bottom lip being pulled between my teeth, and as much as I want to tell him that he's everything I have ever wanted, I can't. "What do you want, Halee?"

"I-I don't know yet, Luke." There's a battle that is taking place inside of me and I can't seem to figure out which side I'm on. My heart knows that there won't be anyone else in the world like Luke Taylor, and that this man in front of me owns my heart. But my head is screaming *he just had another woman in his bed less than a week ago. And not that long ago he said that you weren't enough, your love isn't enough. Walk away.* And as much as I want to throw caution to the wind and say screw it, I know that my heart can't take much more. If I want to potentially have any sort of friendship and co-parenting relationship with this man I need to take a step back.

So that's exactly what I do. "Listen, I think we need to just cool it down a little. A lot has happened recently, and maybe we can continue trying out this friendship thing for awhile. I'm going to take you up on your offer to take a bath, and then how about we watch a movie and eat dinner upstairs in my room?" Shit! I just invited him to my bed. Cool Halee, really smooth. And as if he can see the panic cross my face, the left side of his perfect mouth goes up, exposing the dimple that brings me to my knees. "You know, since I HAVE to be in bed. Doctor's orders right?"

"It's a date."

"No, no… not a date. Just two friends hanging out, eating dinner and watching a movie. That's it." Fuck, fuck, fuck. How am I supposed to resist this man.

My heart shouts, *you don't have to, he can be yours.*

"Whatever you say, princess. See you in about an hour. Holler down if you need something before then." And then he disappears around the corner, back towards the kitchen.

As I make my way up to my room I think out loud, "What the hell have I gotten myself into?"

Chapter 36

Luke

Why the hell did I suggest that she goes up and take a bath? Now, all that is running through my head is the fact that I know Halee is right above me, completely naked and I'm down here making my sisters famous chicken and noodle soup. I have to figure out a way to break down the walls that she has up right now. She knows better than anyone else that we are meant to be together.

Have we both made stupid, reckless decisions, one hundred fucking percent but if there was any doubt left in my mind, it was blown away the minute our lips touched again.

I know that I need to tell her the truth about what she saw the day she told me to leave. But part of me doesn't know why it even matters. Did I sleep with that woman? No. But would I have slept with her if I wasn't so drunk that even my dick couldn't figure out that it was supposed to be hard? Probably.

Annie seems to think me explaining that to her will make everything go back to the way it was before, but I know better. I have caused her so much pain in these past few weeks, I don't think I would blame her if she never let me fully back in again.

✂✂✂

"You dressed?" I tap lightly on her bedroom door.

"Yeah, you can come in."

When I open the door, she's sitting on her bed, wearing those damn yoga pants that she knows drives me wild. But what surprises me is she's wearing a concert tee of mine from the last tour I was on. How did she even get that? "Nice shirt." I nod in her direction as I walk to the nightstand to set down the tray full of food and drinks.

Her cheeks blush, "Oh." She looks down and rubs her stomach over the shirt. "It's kinda the only shirt that isn't tight on me right now. I've basically been living in it for weeks."

"Where did you get it?"

"I ordered it online. I really wanted to go to your last show that was in Ohio, but I didn't know how I would feel, you know, seeing you up on stage again." Her eyes fall back down into her lap and I notice the small infinity symbol that she keeps drawing on her belly. "I know it sounds crazy, but that first night I watched you perform... I'm pretty sure was the night I fell in love with you. And the way that you looked at me, like I was the only person in that bar, I couldn't bear the chance of seeing you look at someone else like that."

"I don't-" I sit down in front of her, pulling her chin up so I can see her crystal blue eyes. "I don't look anymore."

"What do you mean?" I can tell her heart starts to race, and that damn lip. I swear it will be the death of me. I reach forward and pull it out of the firm hold her teeth had on it.

"I don't look at the crowd. I mean I do, but not anyone close to the stage. The first few shows I did, because I swear I just kept looking for you. But after awhile it just hurt, the pain was too much, knowing you weren't out there. Knowing you didn't want me anymore."

Halee lets out a gasp, "Oh Luke! Is that what you think? That I didn't want you?" Now it's me struggling to keep eye contact. She brings her hands to mine and squeezes. "I've never NOT wanted you, Luke Taylor. In fact, watching you walk away from me that night broke me. Knowing you might never forgive me for keeping the truth from you, shattered my soul. But I wanted you to live out your dreams, I still do. I just didn't want to be the reason that you never reached your full potential, and I was nervous if I told you about Bean back then, you would walk away from music altogether. And I couldn't live with that. The idea of you resenting me or our child someday, was enough for me to let you go, with the hope that you would find your way back to us."

"And now that I'm back?"

"I don't know if I can answer that." Her fingers make their way through her blonde ends that are still damp from her bath. "In my head, I had it all planned out, you would walk back in and everything would be perfect. But when you came back I saw that you were different, almost as if you were even more disconnected with the world than you were when you left. And I know I did that to you. But I never imagined for one second you were out on the road, hooking up with groupies, multiple women at a time, and drinking your way through life. And then after you found out the truth, you kept up with that lifestyle."

I interrupt her, "I haven't so much as kissed another woman since the night I found out you were pregnant Halee."

"Luke, I watched you come home as the sun was rising, or even worse, I saw the woman leave that morning. Do you think I'm naive enough to believe she stayed the night with you and nothing happened?"

I look out the window towards the lake, "I'm not saying that I wouldn't have slept with her. I was really drunk. I've basically been living in an intoxicated state since the night I walked out of here. It's the only thing that will even come close to dulling the pain of losing you. But no Halee, I did not sleep with that woman. Apparently, my buddy below the belt couldn't rise to the occasion and she said that I just kept calling her Halee."

We both stay quiet for what seems like an hour, just looking out the window and taking in the sunset. This view, with this woman, is exactly how I want to spend the rest of my life. How do I get her to understand that.

"Where…" "What…" We both finally break the silence at the same time.

"You go first." She says.

"Where do we go from here?"

"I don't know. But maybe we start with hanging out, considering you have already signed up to be my babysitter for the next few weeks. And we can see what happens. No matter what, we're going to be in each others lives." She looks back down at her round stomach. "I guess we just need to find out in what way."

She lays back and I move so I am laying next to her. "Oh my god, Luke, give me your hand." She quickly pulls me so that my palm is resting on her belly. "Do you feel that?"

"Is that?" The small thumping that is happening underneath my hand overwhelms me. I have never felt anything as magical as what I'm feeling right now.

"That's our baby, Luke."

My words are gone. Anything I wanted to say to her in this moment, disappeared. I'm not sure how long we lay just like this, side by side, our only connection is where my hand is touching her stomach.

The sun has completely set, no longer casting shadows throughout the now dark room.

"Tell me a secret rockstar."

I let out a sigh of relief as the familiarity of the situation hits me. "Only if you promise to tell me your secret."

"Deal."

I think for a moment about what I want to say. Part of me wants to tell her I love her and that I'm never leaving her again. But at the risk of pushing her away, I say, "There's nowhere else in the world that I would rather be. Laying here on this bed next to you, feeling our unborn child kick inside of you, this is my dream, Halee. I just never saw it before now."

She is quiet but judging by the way her body is slightly moving, I can tell she's crying. "Halee?"

"I don't want to be your friend, Luke."

"What?" I sit up so my weight is on my one elbow, bringing my other hand up to her face to wipe the single tear that has fallen.

"That's my secret. I don't just want to be your friend. In fact, I'm not even capable of being JUST your friend. I want you. All of you."

A sigh of relief escapes me. "You have all of me… today and everyday for the rest of our lives. As long as you want it, my heart is yours."

Epilogue

Halee

April

Today's the day… the day that ten plus years ago doctors told me would never happen. I'm going to be a mom. The past three weeks have been somewhat of an emotional rollercoaster. Between Luke and I professing our love for one another, giving each other multiple orgasms without penetration, and then him yelling at me saying 'you're so damn stubborn, woman, why can't you just stay in bed like the doctor told you?' we're basically back to being our normal selves again.

One minute we're snuggled up as close as this giant basketball-size stomach of mine will let us, whispering sweet secrets all through the night. And the next minute we are bickering about what show to watch and how he thinks all of the reality TV shows that I choose are crap, and I think the hunting and fishing shows he watches are like watching paint dry. But at the end of the day, this is us. And I wouldn't change anything about it.

Three nights ago, I woke up to the sound of his guitar being played somewhere in the house, so I rolled out of bed and found him in the nursery.

I don't know what song he's playing but it's one of the most beautiful melodies that I have ever heard. I know I'm supposed to be laying down as much as possible but nothing in the world could drag me away from this moment. So here I stand, leaning up against the door frame, watching my sexy as sin man make music while only wearing his boxers.

"Tell me a secret princess..." his voice wakes me out of whatever dreamland I was living in. I didn't even know that the music had stopped.

"I think I'm the luckiest girl in the world."

He sets down his guitar and starts walking towards me. The moon coming in the window behind him illuminates the toned muscles that cover his body. Damn, my man is sexy.

"Well that's not a secret darlin'."

I roll my eyes and slap his arm when he gets close enough. "Oh no? Well how about you tell me a secret then rockstar."

"Fresh out of secrets... but you should be in bed. Come on." He pats my butt and starts nudging me towards our room. Annie and a couple of other friends moved all of his things here last week. And other than running out, once, to the store, he hasn't left my side since he came back. We go to my doctor appointments and then we come home and binge watch 'The Ranch' and eat. Honestly, the idea of having to leave our little bubble of paradise for the real world makes me sad. But I know it's coming.

"Well I would've been sleeping still, but I woke up to one of my favorite sounds. Was that a new song? I don't think I've heard you play it."

He helps me back into bed, then walks around and crawls in next to me. "It's something I've been working on, it's about you and Bean."

"Will you sing it to me? Pleeease?"

"Not yet, it's not ready yet."

"Halee?" My brothers voice pulls me out of my memory.

"Hey Graham, come on in. Luke just ran down to the cafeteria to grab a cup of coffee." I laugh, "Pretty sure he's more nervous about them cutting me open than I am."

My brother smiles, and I can tell it is genuine. I haven't seen my brother smile, like *really* smile, in a long time. Not since he was left heartbroken the day before he loaded the bus for basic training. He claims he's happy with his fiancé Emma, and that he's glad to be back in Iron City after getting medically discharged from the Army. But I'm not one hundred percent convinced, and I'm not sure which part I think he's faking. Emma is a really nice woman. Always perky, kinda overly perky if you ask me, and she's a gorgeous kindergarden teacher with a heart of gold. She screams wife material, but when I look in my brothers eyes, I know something's missing.

"Well I hate to break it to you Hales, but your boyfriend's kind of a pussy."

"Graham! You know I hate that word."

"Sorry, but it's true sis."

We are both laughing when Luke walks back in the door. "What's so funny?" He eyes both of us, knowing that he isn't in on whatever joke was just told.

"Nothing." I say before Graham can reply. I know my brother likes Luke, just like the rest of my family, but he has also been giving him a hard time since everything happened.

"Are we ready to have a baby?" Doctor Johnson makes her way into the room, followed closely by her team of nurses.

"I'll see you guys in a bit." Graham leans down and kisses my forehead, and turns to head out into the waiting area. He slaps Luke on the shoulder on the way by. "Try not to pass out *rockstar*."

We hear his contagious laugh the entire way down the hall.

"Okay Mom and Dad," Doctor Johnson stands at the end of the bed looking at my chart. "Let's go over everything… baby Bean is breach and you two decided to do the cesarean rather than us trying to rotate the baby." We both nod. "Alright, well, Dad, here are your scrubs, get changed and the nurse will bring you in when it's time. Halee, we're going to head in now."

Oh God. This is it. "Okay." My voice shakes as my nerves get the best of me.

Luke leans down, placing the lightest kiss on my lips. "You're going to be great Halee, I'll be there in a few minutes. I love you."

"I love you."

By the time they bring him into the cold, sterile room, they already have me prepped. I'm laying on a table, I can't feel anything below the curtain that's now placed across my chest and all that is keeping me calm is the beeping noise of the machine tracking my heartbeat.

When I see Luke walk in, I feel my heart start to race and my cheeks lift. He leans down and whispers, "Why are you smiling so big princess?"

"Because Luke, we're having a baby."

The sweet moment of his lips being on my forehead is interrupted by the doctors voice. "Okay Dad, we're about to pull out your baby, do you want to watch?"

My normally strong mans face pales and his eyes become the size of golf balls. "Naw doc, I think I'm good with the view right here."

I feel some pulling and then we hear it, the sweet cries of the little person that's going to make our lives complete.

"Congratulations you two, looks like you have a little girl."

Luke follows the nurse over to where she is cleaning up our little miracle and taking all the necessary measurements. When everything is done, she's bundled into a pink blanket and they place the smallest hat that I've ever seen on her tiny head.

I'm not even sure what is happening below this curtain, because the only thing I can focus on is the man across the room who is now holding his little girl in his arms for the first time. My whole life is wrapped up in those two people, and I can't imagine it any other way.

"She has your eyes darlin'." He leans down so I can see the face of the tiny person that has been kickboxing inside of me for the past few months.

She's perfect.

><><><

Everyone has finally left.

Don't get me wrong, I love my family and friends, but they can be a bit much. It's been a big day and all I want is to spend some time with my perfect little family.

"We need to decide on her name." In the past nine months the idea of thinking of names apparently never crossed either of our minds. So the sweet little angel that is cozied up in her daddy's strong arms is currently nameless. "What's your sister's middle name?"

Luke looks up from his pride and joy and gives me a confused look. "Annie? Her middle name is Lauren. Why?"

"Lauren." I say quietly. "I think it's perfect. Lauren Quinn Taylor…"

He looks back down and then his sleepy eyes find mine again, "Lauren Quinn Taylor. You're right, it is perfect. Annie will be pumped."

Luke stands up and lays Lauren down in her bassinet, whispering something that sounded like 'pretty as a peach just like your momma' before he walks away.

"Marry me." He says as he sits down on the edge of the hospital bed.

"What?!"

"Please, marry me, Halee."

"You are tired and full of adrenaline, you crazy man. Let's maybe talk about this at a later date."

"I am not tired, or crazy… I'm in love. With you, with her." He looks over at the daughter that we created together. "Agree to be my wife, raise our little girl together, and spend the rest of our lives bickering about what to watch on tv. I've never been more sure of anything in my entire life Halee. I want you, I have wanted you since the minute I saw you standing in the middle of the dance floor. Be mine. Forever, princess."

He reaches in the side pocket of our overnight bag and brings out a small black box. My eyes blur as I take in the surrealness of this moment. Just over a year ago I would've laughed if someone told me that in the next few months I would not only find my soulmate, but that we would beat the odds and create the most beautiful little girl in the entire world.

Panic strikes as I start to think about how this will all work out. "What about your dreams Luke? Aren't you worried that being tied down to someone like me will just hold you back from reaching your full potential-"

His lips stop my ramble mid-sentence, "The only thing I'm worried about Halee is living a second longer without knowing you will be by my side. Everything else, well, we'll figure it out along the way darlin'. One things for sure, as long as I have the two of you, everything else in my life will be perfect."

Luke opens the small box and inside sits the most stunning ring I've ever seen. "What do you say Princess, wanna take on life with me?"

A smile takes over my face as I realize that I can't imagine it any other way.

"Yeah rockstar, I'll marry you."

He slides the ring on my finger and his lips find mine. Everything that I've ever doubted about us drifts away. We may have taken the long road to get here, hitting every damn Michigan pothole along the way. But I've never felt more at peace with my life than I do right now, in this moment. We may have a lot to figure out, and knowing us, nothing will come easy, but I know for a fact that this man is exactly who I was meant to find. He is the person I've dreamed about finding since I was a little girl… he's my soulmate.

Looks like I was wrong.

This princess does find her prince charming, getting her happily-ever-after, after all.

The End
Until next time… *kiss face*

Acknowledgments

Book two. Crazy.

Never in my wildest dreams did I ever think my writing adventure would get this far.

Quinn & Walker stole my heart when I wrote their story, but Halee & Luke ran away with it. The way these two love, cautiously but fiercely, with one foot out the door while waiting for the other shoe to drop, speaks to me. Although I say that these characters are just fictional, while writing Someone Like Me, Halee and her struggles/insecurities really hit home and pulled at my heartstrings.

Lucky for me, I found my "Luke" when I was seventeen years old, and he has accepted all of my imperfections from day one. Beau Thomas, thank you. You are my rockstar, not only are you the best dad to our mini, but your faith in me, my dreams and your unconditional support makes all of this so much easier. I'm so blessed to have you on my team, I love you, babe.

My Girls aka beta readers! Again, none of this would be possible without you. Thank you for loving Halee & Luke and their story as much as I do. You guys take my first draft, read it, fall in love with it (imperfections and all) and then give me ideas on how I can make it better. For that, I'm forever grateful.

Tammy, Lori & Bonnie... you guys edit my crazy. I said it last time, and I'll say it again- they're the real MVP's.

My parents- I could show up at your house, tell you I wanted to start an elephant farm and even though it might be completely unrealistic, you're going to ask what I need help with. I appreciate the unwavering love and support you two give, and most of all, thank you for teaching me that it's ok to step outside of my comfort zone and try something new.

My readers. A huge shout out to everyone who's on this journey, your kind words mean the world to me. I hope you love Halee & Luke as much as I do and thanks for believing in my dreams. I appreciate you all... more than you know.

Luke & Halee's Playlist

Like I Loved You - Brett Young
On My Way To You - Cody Johnson
(W&Q wedding song)
Middle Of A Memory - Cole Swindell
Take It From Me - Jordan Davis
Kinda Don't Care - Justin Moore
What Ifs - Kane Brown ft. Lauren Alaina
One Number Away - Luke Combs
Meant To Be - Bebe Rexha & FGL
I Hate This - Tenille Arts
Love Me Like You Mean It - Kelsea Ballerini
Lights Come On - Jason Aldean
Stay - FGL
Yours - Russell Dickerson
Stone Cold Sober - Brantley Gilbert
I Don't Know About You - Chris Lane
Best Shot - Jimmie Allen
First Time - Lifehouse
Sorry - Buckcherry
Mad - Ne-Yo
It's Your Move - Josh Kelley

Iron City Heat Series

Someone Like You
(Walker & Quinn)

Someone Like Me
(Luke & Halee)

Coming Soon:

Someone Like Her
(Graham & Lennox)

Connect with Brit.

Instagram:

Instagram.com/Brit_Huyck

Facebook:

facebook.com/authorbrithuyck

Facebook Reader Group:

Brits Book Babes

Goodreads:

goodreads.com/author/Brittni_Huyck

Turn the page for a sneak peek of....

Someone

Like

Her

Prologue

Graham

Lenny: I don't know if I can do this Graham.

I stare down at my phone, reading the words that I knew were coming, but silently hoped wouldn't. I've spent the last four years of my life with Lennox Coleman, and I can't imagine spending any of the next one hundred without her. The year she moved to Iron City was the best yet, I'll never forget watching her walk into our gym class halfway through freshman year.

"Everyone, I would like you to meet Lennox Coleman...", everything else in that moment drifted away when I looked up and saw her face. The way her chestnut hair sat on top of her head in one of those high ponytails, leaving small pieces out to frame her perfect cheeks

and dimples. This girl wasn't like any of the others I went to school with, no, she's real looking. Her beauty isn't masked with caked on make-up, nor is she wearing skin tight shorts, or a barely there tank top.

Instead, her athletic shorts are showing just enough of her tan, toned legs to keep any average male interested, and they're paired with a worn looking Matchbox 20 t-shirt. She clearly has crap taste in music but I suppose if everything else about her is perfect, I can't fault her for that.

"Oh. My. God. What's she wearing?" I glance over to the group of girls sitting beside me, wondering why I continue to surround myself with them. Chelsea's probably the worst, and lucky for me, shes seemed to have staked her claim on me- warning all the others to stay away because apparently I'm 'hers'.

Lennox sits a few feet away by herself, not that I can blame her, the options of friendly faces in this class right now are slim pickings. Besides me, my best friend Jace, and a few of the other guys from the baseball team, the gym's filled with girls who are only here to be close to us.

I stand up and head in the direction of the new girl, "Um... where exactly do you think you're going?" Chelsea snarks as I pass.

"To be a genuinely good human being and introduce myself. Maybe you should try it, you know, being genuine or a good human being." I smirk, raising an eyebrow on my way by.

She mumbles something under her breath, but I don't care enough to turn and ask her to repeat it. I plop down, closer than what Lennox apparently feels comfortable with because as she turns to look at me she slides a few inches in the opposite direction.

"Hey, I'm Graham."

Her cheeks flush as she subtly looks me up and down. Okay, maybe she isn't so subtle about it, but at least she's controlling herself enough to not obnoxiously gawk like the other girls do. "I'm Lennox, which you already know because the teacher just told you. Sorry, I swear I'm not always this awkward, but this whole being the new girl sucks. By the way, your girlfriend looks super pissed off that you are over here with me and not by her."

I turn and look up at Chelsea and her group of minions who all seem to be throwing *eye daggers our way. I laugh, and I pull my attention back to Lennox, "Oh, Chelsea, she's definitely not my girlfriend."*

"Huh. Well, someone should tell her that." She smiles.

Oh, that smile, she could end wars with her smile. Yeah, Lennox Coleman is going to be trouble with a capital T, but I think she's just the right kind of trouble for me.

A slap on my back wakes me out of my memory, "Hey, big bro, where's Lenny? I wanted to show her all of the new clothes I got when mom and I went back-to-school shopping last week." My little sister, Halee, is only two years younger than me but she's the definition of 'baby of the family'. There's a reason we all call her princess.

"She should be here soon." My answer seems believable enough that Halee trots away, joining her best friend Quinn over by the bonfire.

Me: Please Len. Don't give up on us yet. I know me going into the Army isn't ideal but it's what I've dreamed about since I was a kid. Everything's going to be okay, and we'll figure the "us" part out along the way. Please. I need you Lenny.

I sit and wait for her reply. I wish they would invent a phone that had a way for you to see when someone has read your text or even better, when they are texting back. But I shouldn't complain too much, I love that we can text now instead of always having to call or chirp people.

My phone vibrates.

Lenny: I love you Graham, but I have so many dreams of my own and none of them include being married to the military. I just need some time and unfortunately, time is something I don't have. You leave tomorrow.

Me: I know you have dreams, and I know how important it is that you follow them and become a big, badass attorney. I have to get on the bus in less than twelve hours, I hope you change your mind and come to the party. I can't imagine doing it without seeing you at least one more time. I love you, Lennox.

I wait a few more minutes with no reply before I pocket my phone and head over to where everyone else is at. My parent's thought it was important to throw this giant going away party before I left, and at first, I was cool with it. But now, knowing that there is a chance my girl won't be here- all these people are just obstacles keeping me from leaving to go find her.

"Here, you look like you need this." Jace stumbles up, handing me a red solo cup. Being the son of the undersheriff has made him a little less cautious then the rest of us when it comes to stupid shit. Like drinking beer in the middle of the lawn while all of our parents are up on the deck just thirty yards away.

"Dude, you can't even wait until they all call it a night before you start drinking? Are you trying to piss your dad off again?" I set the cup down, a beer sounds great right now, but I need to be one hundred percent on my A-game when Lenny gets here. I have to convince her that we can beat the odds, she has to know that her and I, we were cut from the same cloth. We were made for each other.

"You signed your life away to Uncle Sam, and are getting on a bus to go put yourself through literal hell for the next few weeks... you can have a damn beer, bro." He bends and picks the cup up, handing it back to me. "This is the last time I'm going to see your sorry ass for awhile-"

"Ok, ok." I throw my hands up in defeat, taking the cup back from him before he can go full toddler tantrum on me. "I will drink a beer with you. But for the sake of not making this weird, please don't get all emotional on me. I already have so much going on with Lenny, I don't know if I could handle you weirding out about me leaving too."

We head out towards the end of the dock, stopping about midway to sit and put our feet into the warm August water. Jace seems to be stumbling a little more than I feel comfortable with, so the idea of taking him to where the water is over his head, doesn't seem like a good one.

"Lennox is… well, she's just Lennox. I'm sure she'll come around, you two have basically been inseparable since the day her family moved here. Talking about making things weird though, so your sister and Quinn? Are they both off limits?" His words are a little slurred and I try to take what he's saying with a grain of salt, he knows those two are just as off limits as Lennox is in my eyes. Not only would I kill him, but if I wasn't around to get the job done, my older brother Will would drive back from college and do it for me.

I let out a noise that sounds like a growl, "Jace, don't fuck with me. You know damn well those three are out of bounds for you. Stay in your own lane brother."

He waves me off, "Yeah, yeah… you and your sports analogy are coming through loud and clear. Not only are you shagging the hottest girl in town, but you also are cock blocking me with two of the others. It's cool though…"

His words fade before he can finish his sentence. "Hey, maybe it's time for you to head inside and sleep whatever this is off."

He stands up, quicker than I expected his inebriated body to move, and heads up towards the house after saluting me on the way by. "Okay boss, whatever you say." I watch him slither his way up the lawn until he disappears into the slider door underneath the deck, then I stand and make my way to the bonfire where everyone else is.

Well, almost everyone else.

The pit in my stomach grows larger, as it starts to set in that I may not see the only person I've ever truly loved before I load onto that bus tomorrow. And as I sit and listen to the people who have been in my life for as long as I can remember talk about college classes, dorm rooms, and roommates, I realize that the next few years of my life is going to be dramatically different than theirs. And it suddenly hits me how unfair it's been of me to expect Lenny to give up everything she wants, just to be constantly uprooted and moved around the world at the drop of a hat.

As I sit here, staring aimlessly into the oranges and yellows of the fire, I make a silent promise… If Lennox Coleman doesn't come to me before tomorrow morning, I will let her go.

No matter how bad it hurts, I will let her go because that's what you do right? If you love something, you set it free, with the hope that someday, it'll come back to you.

To be continued...